The Phoenix Clan

The Phoenix is a symbol of contradictions: explosive power and great restraint, vast intelligence and deep humility, immolating self-sacrifice and glorious rebirth. These entwined virtues illuminate the path of Rokugan's most mystical Great Clan, the keepers of the *Tao of Shinsei* and caretakers of the Empire's soul.

The Phoenix Clan is most known for its Isawa family, the foremost of Rokugan's scholars and *shugenja*, mystical samurai who can hear and speak to the spirits. Mountains collapse at their whispered requests, dry rivers are convinced to flow again, plagues are banished, restless ghosts are returned to slumber, and crops flourish in previously barren wastelands. Serving these priests are the Shiba, the Phoenix's lone warrior family and foremost of the Empire's *yōjimbō*, or bodyguards. These warriors study theology and philosophy to better understand and guard their charges from threats both mundane and supernatural. Besides serving as the clan's diplomatic arm to the other Great Clans, the Asako family has a small order of monks to maintain their libraries and keep the *Tao*'s greatest secrets hidden until the world is ready for its truth.

Leading them all is the Phoenix Clan Champion, an exemplary samurai from the Shiba family chosen not through birthright, but by the ancestral sword of the Phoenix itself, Ofushikai. Yet even the clan champion bends a knee to the five Elemental Masters, an arrangement unique to the Phoenix Clan. Whereas other families are led by a single daimyō, the Isawa family follows the wisdom of the five most powerful shugenja among them, each the master of a single element: Air, Earth, Fire, Water, or Void.

I wrote this for Christen, my wife, my love, my best friend.

Cover illustration by Amélie Hutt.

Map illustration by Francesca Baerald.

Color insert artwork by Nele Diel, Shen Fei,
Kevin Zamir Goeke, Pavel Tomashevskiy, and Le Vuong.

ISBN: 978-1-63344-327-3
Printed in the United States of America.

Fantasy Flight Games
1995 West County Road B2
Roseville, MN 55113
USA

Find out more about Fantasy Flight Games
and our many exciting worlds at

www.FantasyFlightGames.com

A Legend of the Five Rings Novella

The Sword and
the Spirits

Fantasy Flight Games

SANPUKU SEIDŌ

KYŪDEN ISAWA

SHIRO SHIBA

KYŪDEN ASAKO

Unicorn Lands

Dragon Lands

Phoenix Lands

Lion Lands

OTOSAN UCHI

Shinomen Forest

Scorpion Lands

Northern Crane Lands

Crab Lands

Southern Crane Lands

The Shadowlands

Islands of Silk and Spice

Rokugan

Chapter One

With a sharp clack, Yūka's *bokken* clattered to the dōjō floor. She crumpled, pressing her hand against her right eye.

Hatsu dropped his own practice weapon and rushed to her side. "Let me see it," he ordered.

Blinking back tears, Yūka revealed the swollen welt across her cheek and forehead. Already the eye was beginning to bruise, a slow spread of midnight purple. "Will it scar?" came her tremulous voice.

The guilt was plain on Hatsu's face. "Why'd you drop your guard? I thought you had it!"

Yūka blinked up at him from the floor. She had nothing to say. Father had warned them not to get too carried away with sparring—that they had an important function this evening and would each have to make an appearance. She felt a hot sting as her eye swelled into a puffy thin slit. Father's anger was legendary; Hatsu would get a tongue lashing for sure. She sniffed, heat rising into her face.

Hatsu's disappointed expression crushed her rapid heart. "You've *got* to get tougher, Yūka-chan. Where you're going, there will be no room for softness."

Yūka started to cry. Her voice echoed through the empty dōjō.

Hatsu's face softened. He kneeled, working his *tenugui*, a hand towel presented to him by his sensei, out of his obi belt. He dabbed her tears like a pecking sparrow. The tenugui smelled like him: sandalwood and pine.

"I'm not strong like you, Nii-chan," she whispered. "If only I had your courage."

He smiled, and the dōjō seemed brighter. "You're stronger than you think, Yūka-chan."

He helped her to her feet as she tenderly palmed her eye. "Sorry for crying."

"That's fine." He placed his hand on her shoulder and made a serious face. "You can cry in the dōjō if you laugh on the battlefield."

Her chest swelled. She nodded. She would do better.

"That's enough for today," he said, going to retrieve his dropped bokken.

"One more." She had reassumed her stance, readying her wooden practice sword.

He grinned, falling into his own stance with proud eyes. "That's my little sister."

Shiba Tsukune opened her eyes. That had been long ago, in a similar place. Now, she had a different name. Now, she was here.

A downward strike disarmed her first attacker. The next strike, up and left, would have severed the arms of the second. She spun and knelt, slashing horizontally at the third, another dispatch. Two more strikes and she was back in her original position, the practice weapons of the final attackers clattering to the floor.

The five students bowed as Tsukune lowered her bokken. Her eyes lifted to an ancient banner hanging from the balcony, the banner of the dōjō, the Order of Chikai. A depiction of the Phoenix *mon* blazed at its center, along with a string of words in the Shiba cipher: *When you are willing to sacrifice anything, only then can you be entrusted with the world.*

She started at the sound of clapping. A young man leaned against the nearby wall, his elaborate silks glowing as he smiled. "You are getting faster, Tsukune-sama."

Tsukune winced at the "sama" honorific. She was not used to it yet. She bowed. "Maybe our sparring is leaving a mark."

"Perhaps I've left several," he quipped with a wink. "But hopefully not."

As he approached, the students touched their foreheads to the floor and backed out of the room, leaving them alone.

"So I *am* improving," Tsukune failed to filter the hope from her voice.

His words slipped into the casual syntax, the dialect of friendship. "You're still pausing at the bottom. In dragon posture, the momentum should carry you back up. Be like a coiled spring."

Her shoulders slumping heavily, Tsukune nodded. She had to do better. "I will chisel this into my liver," she assured him.

He nodded, tucking his hands behind his back.

"Care to spar?" she offered, making her way to the weapon racks. She switched her bokken for a long *shinai*, a bamboo sword for contact practice. "Perhaps today I will finally beat you."

She paused, midbreath, at his plain expression.

"Another time perhaps," he said more seriously. "They're ready."

She stiffened. "Now?"

A nod.

Her grip tightened around the shinai. She drew a breath that did not feel deep enough. "I…shouldn't keep them waiting," she murmured, feeling the steady tap against her rib cage increase in frequency. The first impression was the only one that mattered.

"You're not going like that?" Tetsu inquired.

She glanced down at her sweaty practice kimono and *hakama*. There was no way she could appear as she was.

Tetsu chuckled. "Don't worry. I have something that will fit, and one of my servants is a seamstress. Any alterations won't take long."

She nodded. No breath seemed deep enough to still her jittering limbs.

"Are you nervous?"

The rattling of cicadas drifted in from outside.

She shook her head. "No. I'm fine. I'm ready." She managed a smile and abruptly turned to set the shinai back. "Lead the wa—"

As she turned, her shinai struck the bokken stand with a loud *thwack*. The stand teetered for a perilous moment before a cacophony thundered through the dōjō. Tsukune grimaced at her handiwork, practice weapons scattered across the floor.

"What happened?" came a shout from the doorway. Tsukune froze in the instructor's gaze as he slid open the door. His alarmed face softened into barely concealed exasperation.

Tetsu stepped between her and the instructor. "How careless of me! My apologies."

Guilt pricked Tsukune's heart, but she said nothing.

The instructor waved his hand. "It is fine. The stand was quite old. It would have happened sooner or later."

"I will commission a new one," said Tetsu.

Appeased, the instructor bowed deeply to Tsukune and left.

Tetsu affixed her with a knowing gaze. Sheepishly, she showed her teeth. "I might be a *little* nervous," she confessed.

"One can hardly tell," Tetsu replied.

Tetsu awaited her outside a dressing room, a thin paper *shōji* screen separating them. Tsukune watched his impatient outline through the screen as the handmaid, an older woman with gray-streaked hair, tied an elaborate bow into her obi. The woman rolled the shōji aside, and Tsukune jumped at the loud crack.

Tsukune's patterned kimono were contrasting layers of flame beneath a golden, broad-shouldered *kataginu* embroidered with the mon of the Phoenix. The handmaid's hasty addition, two draping sleeves swinging past her knees and attached with thick visible stitches, proclaimed her status as an eligible young lady. Looking up into Tetsu's appraising expression, Tsukune supposed she looked like some manner of awkward bird.

At last he nodded. "Better. I'm not sure the color works."

The handmaid huffed. "Your red one was disassembled for cleaning, I'm afraid."

Tsukune tugged at one long sleeve and gasped as the cord partially unwound. An exasperated puff escaped the older woman's lips as she corrected it, resewing with deftness in defiance of her age.

"Her hair?" Tetsu asked, regarding her simple ponytail.

"No time," the handmaid replied, finishing the weave.

"What's wrong with my hair?" Tsukune asked.

The older woman chuckled and shook her head, as if the answer were obvious. Tsukune's questioning look at Tetsu's face found no answers.

"It's fine," he decided with a nod. "It's not like she's going to meet the *nakōdo*."

"The jacket shoulders are too long," the handmaid observed.

Tsukune regarded the stiff cloth forming a pointed awning at her shoulders. They reminded her of pagoda roofs, of wings.

"She looks authoritative." She felt his gaze rake her one more time. "She'll need to," he added.

Perhaps, if she were lucky, she would fall into a hole on the way to the council chambers.

Soon, they stood beneath a pagoda roof in the Garden of No Mind. The pink moss carpet swirled around islands of gray stone and bushy trees clustered with off-white loquat blooms. The sun was a gold-plated disk hovering low behind curtains of spotty rain.

"A fox's wedding," she murmured.

"Hm?" Tetsu's hands were tucked behind him.

"That's what they call it when it is raining while sunny. A fox's wedding."

"Who calls it that?"

Doubt swallowed her answer. "They do," she said and fidgeted with her sleeves.

She felt his shadow. Looking up, she met his eyes and froze. Gracefully, Tetsu pinched the cord attaching a swinging sleeve and pulled it free. The silk fell like an unfurled curtain, unburdening Tsukune's arm. He did the same with the other.

"Better?" Tetsu asked.

She flexed her arms in warm sunlight and nodded. In his returned smile, she swore she saw his sensei.

When the rain slowed, they left the pagoda's shade and crossed the pink moss, heading for the base of the sheer cliff overlooking the garden. The stone steps carved into the cliff face were still dry. They climbed in silence, Tsukune dragging behind Tetsu's shadow. The keening trill of the garden cicadas rattled in perfect tandem with Tsukune's heart.

At the top of the steps at the center of the Grove of the Five Masters stood an ancient oak tree, whose roots twisted around the entrance to an ancient stone teahouse with five sides. A depiction of the elements balanced in a circle nearly glowed on the shōji door.

Tetsu slid it open. Beyond the doors of the far wall would be a spiraling staircase that led to a subterranean chamber.

Tsukune held her breath, as if to chain her heart and keep it from escaping. She looked away from the door and at the symbol on Tetsu's shoulder, the emblem of the Order of Chikai, the personal bodyguards of the Council of Five.

"What are they like?" she asked.

"Eccentric. You'll get used to them."

"What should I say? What—"

Tetsu offered an encouraging look. "Bow and show deference. Lead with the left, never the right. When they ask you something, answer honestly. Otherwise, just listen.

"You are here to witness so that, if you are called before the Emperor, you may recall their decisions." His eyes trailed to her sword. "Be confident. Even if you do not feel it, you must try to appear that way."

"So I should be more like you," she joked, her voice wavering.

He stared at her, unblinking, for a long time. "Yes," he finally said. "Like me."

She swallowed hard, pushing aside the sensation that she'd stepped on something he was trying to keep clean and hidden, or had opened a door that he'd meant to keep closed.

His eyes narrowed. "I accompanied sensei to meetings once or twice," he murmured, "but I've never been inside the council's chambers. I've never witnessed a champion's briefing."

He was staring at her sword. Bronze wings formed its *tsuba* handguard, the manta skin–wrapped handle was inlaid with pearls, and its sheath was exquisitely carved from a single piece of wood, as if feathers had simply petrified around the blade. The sword predated the katana, curving only gently, worn edge down in her belt. Every Phoenix Clan Champion, all the way back to Shiba himself, had once wielded it: Ofushikai, the ancestral sword of the Phoenix.

She knew, from his eyes, that he wanted it. That he felt it should have been his—the sword, the position, and the accolades. By all rights, it should have. Tetsu was the scion of the late Phoenix Clan Champion. Ujimitsu's teachings, his lessons, his techniques: they all lived on in Tetsu. That, for his age, Tetsu was the greatest warrior of the Shiba family and most promising among the Order of Chikai was no secret—certainly not among the students of the Chikai Academy, who whispered as much when they believed Tsukune was not listening. The same students spread rumors that Tsukune was not ready, that her appointment had been a mistake or, worse, political maneuvering. A young woman just past seventeen with no accolades would be far easier for the council to control than someone of Tetsu's reputation. Surely Ujimitsu's sword was intended for him.

But the sword had not chosen him. It had chosen her.

"You should go," he said abruptly. "They're waiting." His eyes never left the blade.

She bowed and left him at the entrance, glancing back just before the steps carried her out of sight. He never moved, his silhouette framed by the shōji doorway. Where she went, he could not follow. As she lowered herself into the chamber, she wondered if he would ever forgive her.

"This is unacceptable!" barked Isawa Tsuke. Beneath his fiery eyes, the mon of the Master of Fire nearly glowed on his immaculate robes. "Eju, this personal quest of yours has taken too much of the council's time. Just choose someone and be done with it!"

Tsukune snapped out of her daydream and looked down. Her scroll, for the notes for this meeting, was completely blank.

The ancient Master of Air took a tortured breath. He had the look of a man who hadn't done any eating or sleeping since he was young. "Your suggestion…explains…much."

Tsuke bristled. "You do not mean to imply I have elevated an unworthy student?"

The Master of Earth shrugged, ringing the wooden bells on his winged jacket. "I liked your last one better."

"I am not sure you are in a position to speak on the matter of apprentices, Rujo," quipped Tsuke.

The Earth Master darkened and did not reply.

When Tsukune was a child, she'd always looked up to the Elemental Masters, imagining them as sages whose hearts and minds were always in accord. Ruling the clan since the dawn of the Empire and the day Shiba bent his knee to Isawa, they represented the pinnacle of the priestly craft. Their word was beyond questioning, their judgment always unified. They couldn't be the same people who were shouting at each other around the meeting table in the Chamber of Elemental Mastery.

"Can we return to the matter at hand?" asked Asako Azunami, the Water Master's piercing blue eyes twinkling against the twin waterfalls of black hair cascading from her cone-shaped hat.

"Naturally, Azunami." Tsuke laced his fingers. "Three days ago, Azunami and I attempted to purify a blight in the eastern Shiba farmlands. The water kami were silent; we had no choice but to burn the afflicted crops to contain the disease." The implications on the autumn taxes, and the coming winter, he left unsaid. "In contrast, just today a student attempted to invoke the fire kami and suffered several burns." He shook his head. "Every day, the elemental imbalance grows worse."

"The signs are everywhere," Azunami chimed in. "Floods, droughts, storms—without a doubt, it has spread to the provinces of other clans."

"We...must...act," Eju managed. "For the good...of the... Empire."

"Haste is not wise," Rujo spoke. "We still remember what happened when Kaiyoko-sama attempted to correct the balance by herself. She was the strongest among us, her connection to the water kami unparalleled! Yet even with her insights, her ceremony had no effect."

"I would not say there was *no* effect," Tsuke remarked. "The Crane lands weathered a tsunami, after all."

The Masters paused, then collectively looked at Tsukune. Her face had gone white, and her brush slipped from limp fingers.

"Perhaps refrain from writing that part down," Azunami advised.

Ujina, the Master of Void, sighed. "We learned much about the imbalance from that ceremony, but that would be cold comfort to our allies."

The air grew somber. Tsukune had believed, like so many others, that Isawa Kaiyoko had retired willingly to study the *Tao of Shinsei*. Now, however, hearing this, she was not so sure the retirement had been voluntary.

Rujo broke the silence. "Are we sure there is no precedent? The rise and fall of the elements had always been part of the natural cycle. Perhaps this is no different."

"This has…never happened…before," Eju rasped. "Not even… since the dawn…of the Empire."

Tsuke scoffed. "You should know. You were there, after all."

Tsukune winced as Azunami poorly hid a smirk. Ujina placed his forehead in his hands. "Really, Tsuke. Try to remember your station." For his part, Eju gave no reaction.

"Then what is the cause?" Rujo challenged. "For all our time studying this imbalance, we seem no closer to discerning a pattern."

"Is it not obvious?" Tsuke said. "The kami are offended. For two hundred years, the Unicorn have compelled them with their *meishōdō* techniques, invoking them without suitable offerings in exchange. To those barbarians, the kami are merely spirits to be commanded, not divinities to be appeased. Their ignorance will have repercussions across the lands."

"Little good…has ever come…from beyond the Empire," Eju agreed. "Be it the meishōdō…of the Unicorn…or the sorcery…of the Yobanjin."

Tsukune darkened at the word. Yobanjin were the people dwelling beyond the northern border, descendants of those who would not bow to the Emperor and thus were banished. Now, they were known for making raids against her people—the Phoenix.

"In the end there is little difference," Tsuke pressed. "They are both equally disrespectful of the spirits, too focused on the end result to care about the path chosen."

Rujo regarded Tsuke critically. "I did not realize you were an expert on gaijin sorcery, Tsuke, be it Yobanjin or that of the Unicorn."

Tsuke responded in an even tone. "A sword master cannot hide the root of their techniques from another sword master, only from beginners. Anyone who pays attention will know enough."

The Master of Void spoke, his voice rumbling low. "How fortunate, then, that the Unicorn will show their techniques to the Seppun Hidden Guard, at the Emperor's command."

This silenced the table for a time.

Rujo leaned forward. "Your daughter warned the Seppun, Ujina. The Son of Heaven has decided not to forbid the Unicorn from practicing their arts. That no one is particularly pleased may well speak to the wisdom of his decision. In any case, there is nothing to be done about it now." He sat back, deflated. "Nothing except wait. Wait and watch."

Tsuke's expression spoke volumes of his displeasure.

"Forcing the kami to manifest without offerings could cause unpredictable behaviors," Azunami observed. "However, I do not think we can conclude meishōdō is responsible for the imbalance or Atsuko's prophecy. Not until we better understand the nature of meishōdō."

"You have a better theory?" Tsuke replied.

"Perhaps we are being punished." She looked around the table. "With so many omens, is it possible we have offended the Fortunes?"

Eju thumped a weathered hand. "All the more…reason…to act. Repentance…does not…come first…"

"Repentance for what?" Tsuke shook his head. "If this were divine punishment, then the signs would be obvious. The Fortunes would make it clear where the wrong occurred."

Tsukune spoke before realizing it. "Have we asked the other clans?"

As one the Masters turned, a wall of inquiring eyes.

Tsukune's heart raced, and she felt her palms grow slick, but she could not take it back now. Swallowing, she continued. "They may not have the same understanding of the elements, but their perspectives are unique. The Crane are our long-standing allies; their *shugenja* family, the Asahina, would gladly join forces and share their insights into the stars and oceans. The Lion may be assertive, but they are calculating, too, and can be made to see reason once they understand how the imbalance will affect them." She looked from one face to the next with growing confidence. "If we reach out to the other clans, this challenge could strengthen our bonds with the other shugenja families. With every shugenja family's expertise and perspective combined, the cause of the imbalance might be swiftly discovered."

The braziers popped, echoing through the chamber.

"Tsukune-sama," Tsuke said, leaning on the table to regard her openly, "the Lion have long looked upon our lands with jealous eyes. If they discerned we could not depend on the kami to defend ourselves, do you think they would sit idly by, or would they attempt to take them?"

Tsukune clenched her jaw. "Well…"

Azunami chimed in. "For an herbalist, all diseases are cured with herbs. For one who sets bones, all diseases are cured by realigning bones. In this way, when one chooses a doctor, one chooses one's illness." She regarded Tsukune with visible patience. "Are you so certain multiple specialized perspectives will reveal the truth? Or will more voices mean more noise?"

Tsukune sank in her seat. "I…I had not…"

Rujo shook his head. "If we reveal the existence of the imbalance before we have an answer, the Throne will respond as it did to Atsuko's prophecy. It is better that the Phoenix have an answer before we present the question. To do less would shame the clan."

"At least…she suggested…*something*!" Eju rasped. "This council…seems content…to do nothing…about it!"

As the discussion grew heated, Tsukune lowered her head and made a note not to interrupt a council meeting ever again.

As the Masters rose to leave, the tone of the room transformed. Azunami asked Rujo of his daughter's upcoming wedding. Isawa Tsuke helped the decrepit Air Master out of his seat, nodding at the old man's friendly whispers. Gone were the quips and resentment. They left their hostility at the table. This was the council Tsukune had imagined as a child.

She finally understood: at the table, their masks fell and they spoke freely, but once they left this room, the civility and unity resumed. They assumed the best of one another, regardless of what position the others had argued, or how vehemently anyone had disagreed.

Would this courtesy be extended to her?

Rujo and Tsuke lingered at the bottom of the steps. Washing her forearms in the stream nearby, Tsukune couldn't help but overhear their quiet exchange.

"I was out of line earlier," Tsuke said. "My apologies."

"Do not be concerned. I was foolish to take the boy as my apprentice." He sighed. "Perhaps Tadaka will see reason after the week is done."

She froze at Tadaka's name.

Rujo continued. Tsukune could not see his face, but from his voice, it sounded like he was frowning.

"He thinks I will not go through with it." A curt pause. "He is quite mistaken."

When finally alone, Tsukune sat and stared at Ofushikai in her hands. Her fingers wrapped experimentally around the hilt. Her thin fingers seemed mismatched for it: too frail, not large enough. She stared at the sword for a long time, waiting for something. Anything.

She lowered her lips to the bronze tsuba. "Are you there?" she whispered.

"I am," came a voice nearby.

Tsukune froze, then slowly turned. The Master of Void stood by the table, leaning on a cypress cane.

"Master Ujina!" She made a stiff bow. "A thousand pardons! I did not see you there."

"It is I who would apologize," he replied, then gestured to the side. "Do you mind? I would rather take the stairs, but there are a lot of them."

Tsukune nodded. Hooking his arm, she led him past the lift and up a vast flight of spiraling steps. They walked in silence until they emerged in the sunlit Garden of No Mind. Ujina thanked Tsukune, and they stood watching the pond for a while as the summer breeze stirred the butterburs.

"I spoke out of turn," Tsukune admitted.

"Out of turn, you say." He watched a dragonfly dance with a mosquito.

"It was not my intention to question the council. I only wish to be of some use. I should have said nothing."

"I am glad you said what you did. It needed to be said."

Her face slowly lit up. "Then you agree?" She thought for a moment. "If you mentioned this, it could convince the others. Your esteemed word—"

"I actually agree with the council," he said. "I am just glad you were willing to speak dissent."

"Oh. I see."

He looked up. The sun carved shadows into his wrinkled face. "You are young, Tsukune-sama. You see the world as you wish it to be. You believe involving the other clans will make this matter easier. Sadly, this is not so. It would achieve the opposite." She caught a glimpse of sadness behind his dark eyes. "The other clans may wish the best for the Empire, but they tend to themselves first.

They would seek an advantage, and their games would only serve to make our task more difficult. While it is true that every clan holds a piece of wisdom, this task is only for the Phoenix."

"I understand."

"Your predecessor, Shiba Ujimitsu, was a very proactive champion. It is not well known, but he did not always agree with the council's decisions. Yet he always served. Now, we test our newest champion and wonder what kind of daimyō she will be."

"I've been wondering this myself," she murmured.

A nightingale keened and another answered.

"How is your son?" Tsukune asked suddenly.

"Headstrong and proud. Still."

"I overheard something," she admitted. "I wasn't sure what they were talking about, but they mentioned him."

Ujina sighed. "Yes. An unusual situation. As it turns out, my son challenged Master Rujo to a duel, and Rujo accepted. It shall be settled by season's end."

Tsukune's jaw went slack. "He...he what?"

"A disagreement stemming from his proposal to study with the Kuni. The council declined his proposal, and he blamed Rujo." He sighed again and rubbed his forehead. "You were the only one who could ever talk sense into him, you know. It is a shame you were not there to do so recently."

She clenched her jaw. "Where is he now?"

"He still has a duty to the council, so he was dispatched on an investigation. Some unusual occurrences at Sanpuku Seidō—Cliffside Shrine." He waved his hand. "Worry not. It is in the hands of the Fortunes."

She nodded absently.

"So," the Master said, "you and Ofushikai are becoming acquainted, yes?"

"In a manner of speaking." She glanced at the blade in her obi. "When it lets me."

"Has it spoken to you?"

"It has."

"What did it say?"

She felt as though she were kneeling in the dark before the shrine to Shiba, the weight of a new winged kataginu pressing down on her shoulders, the burden of the clan resting silently in her hands. She remembered that moment, looking into the blade, dozens of faces looking back...

"It said, 'You will never be alone.'"

The Void Master stroked his chin. "Interesting."

"Why me?"

The question surprised her, even though it had come from her own mouth. Ujina regarded her with a patient smile.

"Why me?" she repeated. "How does the sword choose?"

"I cannot say for certain," he finally replied. "Not even Elemental Masters have been able to discern a pattern. The sword chooses as it will."

"It should have been Tetsu." She regretted speaking the words as soon as they left her lips. Her face burned.

Ujina shrugged. "If the sword were meant for Tetsu, it would have chosen him. It did not. It chose you." He regarded her with starry eyes. "If you seek the answer why, look within."

Her hand absently curled over Ofushikai's too-large hilt.

A distant bell rang. It was the Hour of the Serpent. More appointments. Tsukune bowed and excused herself.

She paused and looked back. He was still watching the pond, the Void mon almost glowing white against the dark crimson of the back of his garment.

"Sanpuku Seidō," she called to him. "Where is that exactly?"

From his voice, Tsukune thought he might be smiling. "North. Garanto Province. One would find it on the tallest mountain in the range at the very edge of Phoenix territory." He paused. "Three days' travel. Perhaps four."

"Thank you," Tsukune said and bowed before leaving.

After some time, Ujina smiled at a butterbur leaf where a butterfly dried its dewy wings. His voice was just above a whisper. "We are even now, my friend."

Chapter Two

In the Empire's darkest hour, Shinsei, the Little Teacher, came to the greatest priest, Isawa, for only the magic of his tribe could defeat and bind the fallen god, Fu Leng. Yet, Isawa refused. He could not abandon his people, and without his guidance, what would become of them? So Shiba, a living god, bent his knee before the mortal Isawa, making for him a sacred pledge. If Isawa would agree, if he would join the Seven Thunders, then Shiba's line would serve Isawa's forever...

"This way, Shiba-ue."

Tsukune flinched out of her daydreaming thoughts. The guide gestured ahead with her lantern. She followed, flushing when the guide turned away. She could almost hear Tetsu chiding, *"The Phoenix Champion should focus on the present, not daydream before her vassals!"*

She pulled her straw cloak tight against the sting of icy wind. Elsewhere, the autumn season had brought unexpected warmth, but here at the mountainous northern border, the cypresses were white with powdered snow and the pink orchids were heavy with frost. The road had long abandoned any pretense of having been maintained, comprising just mossy platforms of gray rock amid tall silver grass. If the sun had risen, and the wind had parted the trees just so, she would have had a clear view of the treetops of the Isawa Woodlands, and perhaps even the glittering shore of the Sea of the Sun Goddess south of Castle Shiba.

Her guide paused on a raised rock platform and waited for her to catch up. Tan-skinned and round-faced, the guide was seemingly immune to the cold in a sleeveless white kimono tucked into vermilion hakama.

Tsukune sneezed and dabbed at her drippy nose with a knuckle. "Next time, I will wait until sunrise to climb a mountain."

The guide's chuckle caused her heart to skip, and she awkwardly joined in, reminding herself not to speak her private thoughts aloud.

They continued in silence until they rounded a tight corner. The guide's words dragged with the rural dialect. "Here's the mudslide."

The path beyond the lantern was marred by a wet, brown scar, as if a giant hand had scooped out a chunk of the mountain, leaving only enough crumbling stone and mud for one person to stand upon. "What did this?" Tsukune asked.

"A storm, I think." The guide looked apologetic. "Mountains hate roads, as it turns out."

The guide darted across, pausing to show Tsukune where she should place her feet. Tsukune removed her straw sandals before following, the cold ground stinging her soles.

Halfway across, she felt a breath on her neck. Turning, Tsukune stared into a yawning fissure, jagged with rock and churning with darkness. Beneath the wind's whistling, she heard silver chimes and something close to a whisper…

"Shiba-ue?"

Tsukune snapped back, meeting her guide's confused eyes. She blinked absently for a moment, then nodded that she was all right. They continued, Tsukune uncurling her hand from Ofushikai's hilt, which she had not realized she was grasping.

Tsukune spotted her destination as the sun broke over the ridge: a complex of structures with red, flanged roofs clinging to the mountainside, balanced precariously over a vertical drop. If it had been one of her grandmother's wooden replicas of temple complexes, she'd have been scolded for placing it so close to the danger of the table's edge. Surely any moment it would slide off and into the foggy valley.

An arrow with a humming-bulb tip shrieked a keening whistle, echoing throughout the bowl of the ridge. "They'll be expecting you," the guide said. She gestured toward the dot of civilization on the rocky shelf. "Welcome to Sanpuku Seidō."

A small group of servants offered Tsukune obeisance before a *shinden*-style building near the monastery entrance. A quick thaw in a thermal spring bath, a warm layer of fresh clothes, and then she was standing before a sparse court painted with morning light from narrow windows, gazing at the three men awaiting her on the dais.

Only one returned her look, a middle-aged man in a winged jacket announcing him as the lord of the Kaito family estate and the high priest of the shrine. To his left, a boy closer to Tsukune's age watched the window and adjusted his pointed cap. The third was well past the age of retirement. He sat cross-legged in a seat of honor, deep wrinkles carved into his face, a long pipe tucked into his liver-spotted hand. Tsukune could smell sweet smoking leaf in his pipe's bowl.

The daimyō stood. "Welcome, Shiba Tsukune, daimyō of the honored Shiba. I am Kaito no Isawa Nobukai, daimyō of the humble Kaito vassals. On behalf of my family, I welcome you to Sanpuku Seidō." His head dipped. "I apologize for the state of the road. I trust it was not too much trouble?"

"An invigorating hike," Tsukune replied as she bowed. Her hands felt naked without a gift, even though such a gesture was only required from visitors of lower station.

If he felt slighted, the lord didn't look it. "This is the first time in many decades that a clan champion has walked these halls. Congratulations on your recent appointment. I only just heard."

"Thank you. I will strive to be worthy of it."

Nobukai gestured to the young man. "This is my son, Uwazuru."

The boy gave a graceful bow, holding his cap with slender fingers. "Congratulations, Shiba-ue. It is an honor to meet a fellow servant of the Isawa." His sunny smile warmed his words. "I will see to your comfort while you are here. If you need anything, only ask."

"I am grateful," Tsukune replied. She then offered the old man a smile. "And this is your distinguished father?"

The old man grinned, eyes twinkling. Nobukai flushed. Tsukune's heart skipped, as if she'd tripped over a stone she hadn't seen.

"He is…an honored advisor," Nobukai explained.

"I am Asako Maezawa," came the withered sage's gravelly voice, "a man of little importance. Please take no offense at my slight bow, my lady. These old bones…"

"Worry not," Tsukune said. She imagined his story: here was one who had served his clan and should have retired to a monastery to reflect on the lessons of his life, but instead of accepting *inkyo*, he had chosen to remain in service. Her sensei had always spoken highly of such individuals. "Thank you, honored elder, for your service."

His laughter, choppy and unrefined, startled her. "There is some hope for this new generation after all!"

"Please sit," Nobukai quickly offered. "I apologize for the inadequate finery, but in the mountains, you learn to make do."

Tsukune selected a cushion that afforded a full view of the room. It was one of many *yōjimbō* habits that had made her former job as a bodyguard easier. She set Ofushikai to her right, where it would be harder to draw, as was polite. Servants entered with an iron kettle and poured a fragrant liquid into plain ceramic cups.

"A blend unique to the Kaito," Nobukai explained.

The hot ceramic bit her fingertips, but she pressed her palms against its circumference, soaking in the warmth. "You grow tea this close to Heaven?"

"I'm afraid if something is wanted here, making it is the only solution."

They talked for some time. Nobukai asked of her trip, about the state of nearby provinces, and for news from the Imperial Capital. Tsukune answered what she could. She had not attended many courts, but she knew enough to recognize social rituals. One never spoke of business right away.

"So then," Nobukai said at last, "I must admit, I am both honored and surprised today. No retinue, no messenger. Is anything amiss, my lady?"

A cold breeze pricked her skin. "Not that I am aware of."

"Then to what do we owe the great honor of your presence?"

Tsukune set her cup aside. "While I am honored to visit your esteemed family, I am here seeking one of your guests. His name is

Isawa Tadaka."

The old man's eyebrows rose at Tadaka's name. Nobukai lifted his cup, his hand obscuring his lips. "It must be an urgent message for the Phoenix Champion to deliver it in person. Sadly, his assignment keeps him quite busy, and so far he has refused guests." He sipped, set down his cup, and smiled. "If you relay the council's message to me, I will ensure he receives it."

Tsukune looked from one set of expectant eyes to the next. "There has been a misunderstanding," she said. "I am not here on behalf of the council. My business with Tadaka is…"

She stopped. She'd dropped everything to travel halfway across Phoenix lands, unescorted, for personal business. Beneath their appraising eyes, Tsukune could almost hear their thoughts: *Is this how the Phoenix Clan Champion spends her precious time?* She looked into her tea and saw a confused, foolish girl in a dark void.

"It is a personal matter," she finished. From outside came the nervous chatter of crickets.

"I see." Nobukai glanced at his son, then nodded. "Then please stay the night. Uwazuru will prepare your room. What little the Kaito can offer is at your disposal."

Outside Tadaka's quarters, Tsukune came upon a cluster of shrine maidens sweeping the veranda and casting glances at his balcony. It was time for his daily prostrations to the rising run, Amaterasu-ōmikami. They were hoping for a peek at him. Tsukune's heart sank into her belly. Was it like this every morning outside his window, maidens gathering like iris flowers hungry for the sun? He'd always been handsome, and the most gifted shugenja of his generation. In all the time they'd spent together, he'd never had a lack of admirers. And she'd only been assigned to him…

From their disappointed whispers, she discerned that his mysterious investigation had called him away to the mountain peak. *Damn*, she thought. Now she had time to pass, time the Kaito would doubtlessly think she was wasting.

She spent a short while practicing her morning *kata*, then sat in meditation. Usually, this was enough to still her restless heart. But not today, it seemed. *Maybe I could follow him*, she thought, looking up to where the mountain peak was obscured in thick clouds. He couldn't have gotten far. She might catch up if she left soon.

She shook this notion away. *Don't be foolish. What would they think, the Phoenix Champion chasing after him like that?* Even so, with energy brimming over, she could not just wait here.

Instead, she wandered about the open monastery. Tsukune stepped casually along the mazelike network of rickety bridges interconnecting the boxy structures, her touch light on the cylindrical prayer wheels lining the path cut from the mountain flats.

The Kaito were rustic people, soft-featured, a far cry from the angular faces and pronounced cheekbones common to the Isawa. They conversed in their rural dialect as they worked at the morning chores: sweeping the road, brushing snow from flanged eaves, or disassembling robes for cleaning. On one balcony, Tsukune spotted a few cutting their long hair into bangs, while another wove the gathered hair clippings into tiny ropes. Hair was sacred; these would be burned as offerings to the kami. The villagers' gossip and laughter mingled with their ceremonial movements, friendly teasing, and words of encouragement peppered with intellectual phrases and quotes from the *Tao of Shinsei*.

These are Isawa vassals? They seemed too unrefined, too openly emotional, less academic.

The truth was, she didn't know anything about the Kaito, other than the reputation of the acclaimed Kaito Shrine-Keeper School. Their lives were simple. Like hers had been, once.

A Kaito held her tiny daughter's hand as they passed, the little one grinning as her mother nodded politely, barely pausing in their daily lives. They hadn't recognized Tsukune. Wearing borrowed clothes, and with Ofushikai in her room, there was little about her that would distinguish her from a typical visitor. She felt normal.

She missed that feeling.

The monastery was no larger than a city block, ending abruptly at a stone precipice. A flock of wagtails flitted in an arrowhead pattern above, and Tsukune wondered what it was like to fly like that, far above all worldly concerns.

A volley of arrows arched through her field of vision, over the lip of the cliff and down. Tsukune identified the source, a line of students near the edge readying their bows under the supervision of a gray-haired instructor. In tandem they drew, pointing their arrows at the horizon, releasing together. Tsukune exhaled with them, her breath mimicking the collective snapping of their bows. It seemed like only yesterday that she had stood in a similar line.

The Kaito were vassals of the Isawa. Unlike the Kaito, the Isawa were shugenja, samurai who served physical and supernatural lords both, their souls knitted into the very fabric of the universe. While mere priests blindly repeated rituals to appease spirits, the shugenja knew the hearts of gods. They practiced *shugendō*, the prayers that could invoke the manifestation of spirits. To speak to and hear the kami, to ask for favors in exchange for offerings, was a gift only one in a thousand souls ever possessed.

However, while this gift offered shugenja considerable power over the elements, power that could be turned to martial ends, shugenja were sworn to peace. The Isawa did not carry weapons and fought only as a last resort. The use of the kami's blessings for violence was a distasteful notion. The more violent the emotions in a shugenja's heart, the more dangerous the spirits they invoked, until eventually the shugenja's prayers were answered not by kami, but by *kansen*, the corrupted spirits of Hell itself.

Another volley of arrows sailed overhead. Kaito were neither shugenja nor warriors, so what were they, exactly?

Beyond the monastery's edge, across a ravine, stood an ancient shrine. With fiery red columns and interlocking wooden beams holding up a stack of slanted roofs and a bell tower protruding from the eastern side, it looked hundreds of years older than the monastery, and perhaps just as large. A long, rickety wood-plank bridge crossed the harrowing drop of the ravine. The bridge deck rested not on ropes, as she'd initially thought, but on live wisteria vines woven together and rooted on either side. She crossed without pausing, her hand remaining on the handrail vine until her foot touched the other side.

At the outside pavilion, Tsukune ladled water over her hands and rinsed her mouth, then left her sandals on a little wooden shelf. The shrine's stone floor was cold against her bare feet. The rolling canvas walls opened onto a wide veranda overlooking the entire mountain range. Dozens of paper streamers hung low from the rafters, stirred by a lazy breeze, giving the impression of floating ghostly strands. A knee-high fence separated her from a wooden stage that extended to the back. Behind closed shōji doors would be the inner shrine and the sacred artifacts of the Kaito. During worship and festivals, these screens would be cast aside to reveal the objects of worship, like props on a kabuki stage.

That area was off-limits to non-priests. For her to step beyond the screens was forbidden.

Her barefoot path led her around to a cloistered garden. There she found a row of seven tiny shrines, like birdhouses, each elevated to shoulder height on a wooden pole.

She stopped at one with an indigo roof and a cloth bag swaying from its little porch. Kneeling before it, she withdrew a small offerings bag and produced a cone of incense and a pinch of salt mixed with ground barley. She laid these in an installed dish. It was not pure salt, and she could not light the incense, but this would not offend the Fortune of contentment. Taking her prayer beads, she clapped her palms twice and bowed.

"Hotei-no-Kami," she whispered, "I humbly beg your attention."

But when she closed her eyes, she saw the crimson, wind-torn robes of a man whose life she'd sworn to protect, his knees sunken deep into frigid snowbanks, his jagged breath frozen on blue lips. Alone and near death at the mountain peak. With no yōjimbō.

She sighed. The gesture was futile; there was no room in her heart for the Fortune to dwell.

A voice drifted into the garden. Tsukune thought she was imagining it at first, but as it grew in strength, she realized it was singing. It was unpracticed, but bright and silvery, like a rustic bell. She'd never heard a voice so beautiful, not even at the Setsuban festivals of her youth. Her concerns forgotten, she followed it back into the shrine.

A young woman in *miko* trappings was sweeping the veranda floor with a cane-handled broom. Tsukune noticed a splotchy discoloration on the girl's face, spreading from her brown eyes to the bridge of her nose. She sang as unabashedly as a *mejiro* bird, her black ponytail bobbing in rhythm. Unnoticed, each note plucking invisible strings in her chest, Tsukune stood at the door and listened.

Night always falls first
Inside the valley
The sun is eager
It is always diving down

We two are like moths
Chasing the round moon
If the sun won't watch
Then we cannot trust ourselves

Night always falls first
Inside the valley
If not for that hill
We would have a bit more time

The broom clattered to the floor.

"Sorry!" Tsukune said. "I did not mean to startle you!"

Her face flushing, the girl laughed. "Serves me right. I should be more mindful."

"I did not want to interrupt." Tsukune smiled cautiously. "That's a beautiful song."

The girl awkwardly retrieved her broom. "Thank you. My grandmother used to sing it for me. It's an old song." She bowed. "I am Kaito Kosori."

"Shiba Tsukune." Her titles formed on her lips: *Phoenix Clan Champion, Daimyō of the Shiba Family, Protector of the Council, Keeper of the Tao…* Kosori made a toothy grin. The girl, like the others, did not know who she was. She felt normal. So she swallowed her titles, saying nothing more.

"Well met, Tsukune-san," said Kosori. "What brings you to Cliffside Shrine?"

"I came to see Isawa Tadaka."

"Ah, of course." She leaned on her broom. "He left this morning for the peak, alone. Wouldn't let anyone accompany him. He doesn't care much for advice, it seems." She sighed. "The handsome ones never do."

Tadaka clinging to a stone outcropping, a fragile red flame in an icy landscape. His foot slipping. The wind tearing away his voice.

Kosori's smile faded. "Oh. Sorry. I upset you."

Tsukune forced a smile. "It's fine. He *is* stubborn. Always has been."

Kosori looked at her sideways. "Are you and he…?" She crossed her fingers.

"No," Tsukune blurted. "Our fathers were friends. I was his yōjimbō for a time." She watched two moths dance around the broom. "But not anymore."

"I understood a Shiba yōjimbō served her change until death."

"Not always," Tsukune whispered.

Kosori clicked her tongue. "Ah, my dumb mouth. Forgive me. It isn't my business." She looked away. "I should return to my work. Whatever is not finished today will mean more for tomorrow."

She pushed dust with her broom, avoiding Tsukune's gaze. Her feet dragged with her submissive gait. There was one like her at every dōjō. Someone whose purpose was to be at the bottom, the example, the one they whispered about and looked upon with pity. More servant than student. For a brief flash, the shrine became a dōjō in the lands of the Lion Clan, and it was Tsukune pushing dust beneath a hot face and her peers' snickering.

"May I help?" The words came unbidden, but the moment they left her mouth, she found that she desperately wanted to do anything but be alone with her thoughts.

Kosori cast her a skeptical glance. "You want to do chores?" Her eyes narrowed. "You're a guest. It would be unseemly."

"I've heard cleaning a shrine is good luck." She smiled sheepishly. "I could use some."

"I'm pretty sure it was a lazy priest who first said that," Kosori joked. She looked around, then offered Tsukune the broom. "Just don't tell anyone. I'd get another tongue-lashing."

Tsukune bowed as she accepted. "I'll consider it a favor."

Kosori again offered her toothy grin. "Oh? Maybe I'll let you do all my chores and you can owe me another!"

Chapter Three

The time passed quickly, Tsukune's troubles falling away amid the comfort of familiar chores. Kosori sang as they worked, and Tsukune swept to the graceful lilt of her voice. Had Kosori been born in the city or among the court elite, surely she would have been classically trained to sing for daimyō. Kosori scrubbed at a stain with a willow-bark brush. Her path, like Tsukune's, had been decided by fate.

Tsukune swept these thoughts outside with the dust, whispering, "Bad spirits out."

"You've done this before," Kosori remarked.

"I used to sweep the dōjō all the time. We all did. It taught discipline."

"Ever clean rafters?"

Tsukune followed Kosori's eyes to a thick network of cobwebs resembling trapped smoke. She paled. "When was it last cleared?"

"Yesterday." Kosori chuckled at Tsukune's surprise. "I know. We have some diligent spiders. But so be it; shrine spiders are good luck."

Looking up, Tsukune's attention snagged on a massive rope swinging above her in the doorway. It was fraying near the center, the hemp strands protruding in a short tangle.

She darkened. "This *shimenawa* is frayed."

Kosori went serious. "Let me see." She gingerly tested the rope, holding up a vertical hand and whispering an apology to the spirit the rope appeased. Then she drew a small scrap of paper from her obi and affixed it to the tear. The tangled kanji on the surface vexed Tsukune's eyes.

"This rope dates back centuries," Kosori explained. "I've worried about it for some time."

"When will it be repaired?"

Kosori bit her lip. "It'll likely be replaced." She looked as though she might say more, but then shook her head. "In any case, this will have to last until the replacement can be procured."

Tsukune's eyes lingered on the tag for some time.

The midday meal was a bowl of rice and a heap of mountain cabbage. It was shredded, salted, and flattened between rocks until the water pressed out and the leaves were shriveled and tender. They took their lunch to the bridge and sat with their feet dangling off the edge. As they ate, Kosori pointed out villages and way stations beneath them. She held her chopsticks with her hand close to the tapered end, like a farmer or fisherman. Tsukune held hers closer to the back.

Kosori pointed at a thin column of smoke in the distance. "That's a Yobanjin settlement."

When the Empire first formed, there were some who would not swear fealty to the Emperor. These banished people became the Yobanjin tribes populating the plateaus beyond the borders. A Yobanjin could be killed on sight for even stepping into the Empire.

"It must be close," Tsukune remarked.

Her expression faded. "When I was twelve a bunch of them raided the villages. It took weeks to restore the shrines they desecrated." Her hand gripped a vine. "Some villages have yet to recover."

"Do Yobanjin incursions happen often?"

Her eyes narrowed at the distant smoke. She didn't answer.

Tsukune lowered her bowl. "I saw some Yobanjin once."

Kosori regarded her with rapt attention. "Did you fight them?" A smirk cut into her cheek. "I heard they fight like demons."

On the western edge of Phoenix lands was a village whose

name Tsukune had sworn to forget. She would never have known it existed had she not accompanied Tadaka there, breathing tensely as she watched five men for any hostile twitch. They stared through wooden masks, all except for their leader, whose hairy arms rippled out of his stiff tunic, teardrop-shaped earrings clacking around a tattooed face as he argued with Tadaka in a choppy tongue. They barked back and forth until Tadaka added two bolts of silk to the white bronze bars and a jar of powdered cinnabar. In turn, the man surrendered a fibrous scroll to the table. Only after they were gone with Tadaka's offerings did he scoop this up.

The knowledge within that scroll was priceless. This meant it was an unfair exchange to the Yobanjin, and therefore not a violation of Imperial decree, which defined "trade" as "fair exchange." So Tadaka had explained.

Focused on the past, she forgot the present. A chopstick slipped from her fingers, vanishing into the needle-thick canopy far below. She grimaced.

"You can have mine," Kosori immediately offered. "I can just—"

Tsukune snapped her remaining chopstick in two, then resumed eating. Morsels slipped through her weaker grip until she held the bowl to her mouth and shoveled.

Kosori watched with amusement. "You're a determined person, aren't you, Tsukune-san?"

"It's better to carry on," she said around a mouthful.

Finishing, they returned to the shrine for the last of Kosori's chores. Their progress dragged, but with Kosori singing and joking, Tsukune did not mind. The sun gilded the mountain range by the time they finished. "One final chore," Kosori said, dragging the screen walls shut. "The evening blessing."

"How can I help?" Tsukune asked.

She gestured toward an offset hall. "There's a room with some *yumi*. Bring me one and an onion-bulb arrow. I'll meet you here momentarily."

"You need a bow for an evening blessing?"

Kosori's bright affirmative nod banished any notion of jest.

The room was tucked to the side of a long hall near the garden. Asymmetrical bows of varying lengths leaned against a vertical rack, enough to line the entire wall. Some appeared quite ancient, the wood glossy and polished by countless fingertips. Tsukune selected the one she thought best for Kosori's height. Even when strung, it would tower over her.

The far side of the room afforded a view of the garden from a circular window. Tsukune froze in front of it, her eyes narrowing. The cypress beyond wore a blessed rope like a belt around its trunk. Affixed to this rope was a scrap of white, the black letters painful to behold.

Another one? Tsukune frowned. How many of the shrine's blessed ropes had these affixed tags? She remembered how swiftly Kosori had produced one for the rope hanging above the entrance. She'd been concerned, but not surprised. Were all the shimenawa falling apart?

Tsukune returned to the main room with heavy steps. Amber light filtered through the canvas, digging shadows out from every wrinkle in the wood. The paper streamers hanging from the ceiling looked yellow and splotchy in that light. Her nose wrinkled at the dust motes hanging in the stale air. Hadn't they swept and dusted all day?

A faint whistle stirred her ears. The streamers rustled like brittle leaves. The fine hairs on Tsukune's arms stood straight. The streamers undulated, then paused. She heard whispers—faint, distant, but unmistakable.

She brushed her hair away from her ears, slackened her jaw, and closed her eyes. The sound came into focus, wordless and nondirectional. A wheel in her belly turned, instinct spiking her in a specific direction. This was her *haragei*, her belly feeling. A yōjimbō trusted it above all other senses. She opened her eyes. She was facing the stage and the closed screen, behind which sat the inner chamber and the artifacts of the family, as in all other ancestral shrines.

Only priests could venture in there. By tradition, all others were forbidden.

But wasn't she the Phoenix Clan Champion? Tsukune bit her lip.

Stepping over the knee-high railing set her heart at a gallop. She crossed the stage like a child sneaking into her parents' room. The painted screen doors depicted a woman in the garments of a shrine maiden wielding a bow like a thin crescent moon. Tsukune felt the painting's eyes as she brought her ear to the seam between the closed screens. Multiple voices were talking over one another. She knew none of the words.

She pressed her palm into the textured paper. Just a gentle push and it would roll aside. No effort at all. Her cheek pressed against the screen. She held her breath.

"Tsukune-san?"

An icy jolt. The whispers were gone. The stale air, the dust, the sickly bronze light: all vanished. Everything was as it was before. She froze for several moments before turning into Kosori's uncomfortable gaze below the stage. She'd donned a padded chest protector and a three-fingered glove. She stared as though Tsukune had stolen a kami's offering.

Tsukune pushed guilty words through clenched teeth. "This… looks bad. Doesn't it?"

Kosori limply nodded.

Climbing down from the stage, Tsukune kept her eyes on the floor. An avalanche of excuses thundered through her mind. But what could she possibly say? Words seemed too brittle. What would Tetsu say? *He wouldn't have done it to begin with…*

"I won't tell," Kosori said, interrupting her thoughts. Then, as if nothing were awry, she looked pointedly at the screen. "Interesting tapestry, isn't it? It's quite old."

Tsukune stood in the coldness of her guilt. Kosori was inventing an excuse, allowing her to save face. She felt like a fish that had been thrown back from the net. "I've never seen one like it," she managed, looking grateful.

"That's Isawa Kaito," Kosori explained. "This shrine is in her honor."

Isawa Kaito. That would be the founder of the family. The woman on the painted screen drew her bow against a massive ogreish creature. Time had faded both their faces.

Outside, Kosori strung the bow with an ease that defied her spindly arms. Tsukune watched with growing fascination as she nocked an arrow with a felted onion-bulb tip, bracing the massive bow against her knee for support. "I've only seen the arrow readied with the bow held vertically," Tsukune remarked.

"That is certainly more serene. But it forces one to turn the handle, which can weaken one's grip." Kosori brought the bow up above her head and paused. "A weak grip is distracting. If the mind is not on the target, then the arrow will go elsewhere. One must become an empty vessel in which the kami can dwell."

She shifted, pointing the arrow at the shrine's bell. A prayer tumbled from her lips.

Tsukune squinted. "That's perhaps five hundred *shaku*, and you're shooting in cold weather."

Kosori brought the bow to eye level, drawing the arrow to her cheek, the bow's maximum draw. Its mulberry and bamboo strained and bent until Tsukune felt Kosori's *ki* roaring like a wave desperate to break. She exhaled. The arrow launched, the force of the snap spinning the bow in Kosori's hand.

The bell rang. Birds took to the sky, their black silhouettes like inkblots on a firelit canvas. Kosori remained in her release posture. The chime echoed through the valley.

"All things considered," Tsukune said as they walked the grounds, "walking up with a mallet would have worked as well."

Kosori chuckled. "Perhaps. But the kami prefer it this way."

"Is that so?"

Kosori's bashful gaze lowered. "You're the first outsider to see my shot, you know. Flawed as it is."

"Flawed?" Tsukune reeled. "I've known bushi twice your age who could not make that shot!"

"Any success belongs to my sensei." But her smile lingered.

The stood at the cliff's edge. The mountain range unfurled horizontally before them like a vast scroll. It was already night in the shadow-strewn valley, crickets singing among the pinpoints of light marking scattered villages.

"To aim is a delusion." Kosori said suddenly. "The arrow knows the way. So it is said."

"So," Tsukune said, "it is shugendō."

"It is for the kami, if that is what you mean." She faced the sun. "In ancient times, the bow was considered sacred. An arrow can divine the weather. A bowstring's twang can banish evil spirits. Is it so strange that my family would hold the yumi in such high esteem?"

"I have known many Isawa, but none that venerate *kyūdō*"

"Kyūdō holds a place in all the Kaito family's traditions. Through practice, we grow closer to the kami and learn to sense them. And we use kyūdō in defense of Cliffside Shrine." She met Tsukune's eyes. "This shrine marks where a demon was felled by the arrow of Isawa Kaito herself."

"I haven't heard that story."

"Isawa Kaito was the first shrine keeper. All our techniques are derived from her insights. She did not have the shugenja's gift, but she knew how to consecrate a shrine and make herself a vessel for spirits. When she drew the bow, the kami would flock to her and guide her shots. One day, a demon came from the north, destroying villages and scattering helpless innocents. Kaito faced it alone, armed only with her bow and a handful of arrows. With the kami's help, she defeated it, giving her life to seal it away inside a well. When she died, the kami froze the well, trapping the demon inside. This shrine was erected in her memory. Ever since that day, our family trains shrine keepers, preserves Isawa Kaito's ways, and protects this shrine—just as she did."

Kosori stopped, eyes widening, then bowed. "Isawa Tadaka-sama! What brings you to the shrine at this hour?"

Tsukune's back went stiff. Isawa Tadaka stood just behind her, his amused expression nearly swallowed in the shadow of his cone-shaped hat. Broad-shouldered and well-muscled, he towered over them both.

"I'd heard Tsukune-sama was looking for me," he remarked. "I didn't want to keep the Phoenix Clan Champion waiting."

Tsukune shut her eyes. *Damn it.*

At first, Kosori did not seem to understand. But in the numb silence that followed, realization overtook her confused expression, which moved halfway to a grin by way of panic. "Ch-champion?" She stared at Tsukune. "You're the…"

What would be the point of explaining herself now? The damage was done. Tsukune stepped between them. "Thank you, Kosori-san, for keeping me company today."

Humiliation painted Kosori's features. "…Of course," she replied.

Tsukune watched her go, her lungs emptying into a sigh. She turned to Tadaka, who was blinking in confusion. If she could have set fire to his robes with her glare, she would have.

"She didn't know?" He arched an eyebrow. "You didn't tell her?"

"It didn't come up."

He folded his arms into his billowing sleeves, the gesture

making his shoulder muscles ripple in a way that made her heart skip a beat. "My apologies," he said. "Although one might wonder why you would keep that secret." He smiled with his eyes. "It's good to see you, Tsukune. It has been a while."

In fact, it had been months. An entire season, come and gone. No letters. No visits. She'd been his bodyguard, his shadow, for almost a year and then…nothing. *Say something,* she thought. *Tell him you missed him.*

"We need to talk," she said. His eyes dimmed. She inwardly grimaced. *Nice job.*

"Then let's talk." He brushed past her, making for the shrine. "But I'm in the middle of my investigation, so if you have something to say, come along."

Her jaw clenched at the Phoenix crest embroidered on his back. Since the founding of the clan, the Isawa had led and the Shiba had followed. Now would be no different. She sprinted to catch up.

Tadaka paced the belfry, his hand rotating each polished orb of his prayer beads. He did that whenever he was thinking. He always had, for as long as she'd known him. He brushed the ancient bell, nostrils flaring as if following a scent. Then he moved to the banister, at the gap where the broken wood parted like a toothy maw. It made Tsukune's eye twitch. She wanted to pull him back. It wasn't safe so close to the edge.

"Here," he said. "She died in this spot."

"Did a spirit tell you that, or was it the broken railing?"

He smirked and pointed over the side. "If the fall were what killed her, then she would have died down there. Her vessel was empty before it touched the ground."

Which meant she—whoever *she* was—had died before she fell.

"Look at this place," Tadaka chided, tucking away his beads. "Ropes fraying, banisters breaking. And the filth!"

Jerking movement caught Tsukune's attention. A glistening centipede, its black body the length of her forearm, with dozens of red legs, clung to the wall inches from Tadaka's shoulder. Seeing it, he extended his hand. The creature crawled onto his palm. Tsukune's skin pricked as he craned the segmented beast over the balcony and onto the roof, where it crawled away.

"I suspect the Kaito daimyō will not like the report I am giving to the council," he said.

"Does the council usually take an interest in accidents at rural shrines?"

He cast her a knowing look. "The victim was Isawa Iwahaki. Lacking the aptitude for the Isawa Elementalist School, she was sent here to train as a shrine keeper. Her death might have been overlooked but for a letter sent to Master Rujo."

Tsukune blinked. "A letter?"

"Anonymous. Signed with a moniker: Hototogisu." Lesser cuckoo. "So now we are here."

"Now *you* are here," Tsukune corrected. "Doing the job of a lesser council agent."

Tadaka shrugged. "It is an honor to serve the Masters in any capacity."

He was deflecting. She let her irritation show. "Will it be an honor to duel one?"

His eyes lit slowly, and he nodded. "Ah. So that's why you've come." He leaned against the wall and crossed his arms. "Go on."

"He's your sensei!" she blurted. "It's disgraceful! What do you hope to gain?"

"I have reason to suspect the elemental imbalance is connected to recent attacks on the Kaiu Wall. If the Phoenix are to correct this, *someone* must study the Shadowlands."

Tsukune grimaced. To even speak the word was taboo. Nothing good ever came of mentioning the place where the twisted realm of evil touched all things.

Tadaka continued. "They would have recognized the wisdom of my proposal had my master not opened his jealous mouth."

"The Master of Earth is jealous of *you*?" Tsukune scoffed. "Do you hear yourself?"

"It is not hubris if it is true." His handsome face darkened. "For years, Rujo has taken credit for my research, presenting my findings as his own, and I said nothing. Only now that my deeds threaten to overshadow his own does he suddenly have a mind to protest!"

"He is your sensei!" Tsukune protested. "He taught you!"

Tadaka smirked. "I learned plenty on my own. When I defeat him, he will have no choice but to endorse my research. With the council's blessings, I will travel to Crab lands and learn the secrets of the Kuni shugenja. If the worst happens, the Phoenix will be ready."

"And if he defeats you," she said, "you'll be tossed to the winds. No one will even remember your name."

He didn't flinch. "That is not my destiny."

"What happened to you, Tadaka? You were always inquisitive, but you used to be humble. What changed?"

"The world," he replied. "We must change with it or be left behind."

Tsukune stepped forward. She grasped his sleeve. Her voice was almost a whisper. "I can't let you. Some doors are better left closed. Forget the proposal. Apologize to Master Rujo. I'm asking you to let it go. For me." She met his eyes. "Please."

His expression softened. For a moment they just stood there, he looking down at her, she looking up at him.

His eyes closed. "You cannot protect me, Tsukune. You are not my yōjimbō anymore."

Not his yōjimbō. Like a hammer, it split her heart in two.

"You think I wanted this?" She shouted at his back. "You think I did this on purpose? Your father said the sword chose me. Was I supposed to say no?"

He paused in the doorway. The last rays of the sun cast her shadow across the floor, as if it were reaching for him.

"We had plans," he said. "You could have said *something*."

Then he was gone. From the valley, the tangled screeches of roosting birds reached out and choked the serenity from the night.

Chapter Four

The rolling screen doors were cold against her palms. On its painted surface, a woman with a wooden face held the crescent moon in her hands. Tsukune's breath stirred the dusty shrine air and rattled the dry streamers hanging from the ceiling. The whispers on the other side slipped through the crack between the screens. She threw them open. A tsunami crashed through, flooding the world and breaking her.

She jolted. She was lying on a thin futon in a guest room. Outside the circular window, the night hummed. She exhaled slowly to lessen the hammering of her heart. A dream. Jumbled images falling from the dusty cupboards of her mind. Nothing more.

The night breeze chilled her. She made to tighten the collar of her sleeping jacket, but stopped when she felt an object in her fist. She sat up. Ofushikai rested in her clenched hands. Moonlight glinted along the carved feathers of its sheath. It had been on its stand when she went to bed. Had she taken it in her sleep?

They need you, Tsukune.

The words came unbidden to her mind, the voice not her own. She'd heard it once before in the shrine to Shiba in the presence of gossamer reflections…

She drew. A ringing note pierced the night.

The weightless steel was a band of light in her hand. Its curve was less noticeable than that of her mother's katana, the steel slightly thicker, but its flawless edge and mirrored surface defied its thousand years of age. She met her reflected eyes in the blade.

"Who needs me?" she asked. Then, "Should I stay another day?"

Outside, a cold wind ran invisible hands through evergreens and the banners of the monastery.

She sighed, feeding the blade to the sheath once more. "You said I would never be alone. So why do I feel more alone than ever?"

In the circular window, the pale moon watched her like a giant eye.

"Were you able to speak with Tadaka-sama yesterday?" Nobukai spoke without looking down from his seat on the tall stone.

"I was," Tsukune affirmed. With her back against the maple's trunk, she could watch three of the cloistered garden's five corners.

Servants brought the midday meal: a bowl of hot rice, a cup of clear broth, a dish of red pickled radish and cabbage called *fukujinzuke*, and a raw egg. Tsukune followed the daimyō's lead, cracking the egg directly into the rice and stirring this with chopsticks.

"I am extending my stay." She winced. "Assuming that is no inconvenience."

"None at all!" Nobukai replied. "You may stay as long as you'd like."

She watched the rice's heat softly cook her egg. "It will only be until Tadaka-sama's investigation is done."

"Ah yes. The girl." He sighed. "Tragic accident. She was a talented student, if headstrong. She was warned that the winds here could become unexpectedly strong."

Tadaka's words from the prior day echoed in her mind. *Her vessel was empty before it touched the ground.*

"It looked like she broke the belfry banister," Tsukune said.

Nobukai paused. "So you visited the shrine! I trust my niece did not chew off your ear?"

Tsukune hesitated. His niece? The only person there was…

A breeze rattled the purple leaves, revealing a hint of more sky. "So Kosori-san is your niece," she said.

"She didn't mention it?" He shrugged. "Yes. Her mother passed when she was very young. I took her in and raised her with my son."

"She impressed me," Tsukune said. "She taught me much of your ways. Her archery skill is commendable. And her voice…"

Nobukai's eyes shined proudly. "Kosori has her mother's voice. She was always singing as a child. We called her Little Hototogisu."

Tsukune's heart skipped. Lesser cuckoo. The moniker on the anonymous letter that Tadaka had mentioned. Curious.

"Perhaps you could see her again," Nobukai encouraged. "Your studious nature and respect for your elders may rub off on her."

His tone made Tsukune feel like a cat stroked in the wrong direction.

"I have some concerns about your shrine." The words came so suddenly, she wasn't entirely certain they were hers.

Nobukai stirred his food. "Oh?"

Once, Isawa Tadaka had led a tense negotiation with an easily offended Lion Clan samurai. Tsukune had listened from the other side of a paper screen, just close enough to intervene. She never had to. Tadaka's language had been careful. *How would he say this?* She gathered her thoughts.

"The shrines of southern provinces are exposed constantly to sea air. Due to the weathering effect, it has become custom to rebuild a shrine around its inner sanctum every century. Yet the wood and stone of Cliffside Shrine is as if it has never been replaced."

"Quite perceptive." Nobukai nodded. "I would expect no less of a Shiba yōjimbō."

"And of course, when shimenawa are frayed, they are swiftly replaced. So I have heard."

Nobukai set down his food. He was no longer smiling. "You heard correctly. Our own blessing ropes are ancient, dating from the shrine's dedication. I fear ours will soon break, and then the kami will have one fewer place in which to dwell."

Tsukune's eyes narrowed.

"You are not the first to suggest this, Tsukune-sama. If I had had my way, the shrine would have been rebuilt and the blessing ropes replaced the moment I became daimyō." He paused. "As it so happens, those ropes were created and blessed by an Elemental Master. The spirits have become accustomed to them, and so nothing less could replace them. As for the shrine itself, I needn't mention the expense, nor the challenge in transporting materials all the way up here." Another pause. "I mentioned this to the council, and although it has been some time, I am sure they are still considering."

The grass bent to the wind. Tsukune sat back. "I could mention it the next time I'm there."

Nobukai's face brightened. He dropped from the rock and pressed his forehead into the grass. "Thank you!" he said. "We would be eternally grateful!"

Tsukune blanched, wilting, looking anywhere but at the prostrated man before her.

As he rose, his eyes fixated on something behind her. Her instincts spun Tsukune in the same direction. A small, bulbous knob shook beneath a butterbur leaf, something inside stirring, the surface clear like glass. From within, a butterfly broke free, its sky-blue wings unfurling as it crawled to the arch of the leaf. Tsukune gasped.

"Exquisite," breathed Nobukai. "Such sights were rare in my grandparents' time, but our summers are longer now." He raised a reverent hand. "The wonders of the Empire are without number."

The little thing fanned its dewy wings.

"Of course," Nobukai continued, watching Tsukune, "its transformation must confuse it. Its whole life it was only a caterpillar, so close to the ground. Now it must be a butterfly."

Tsukune felt like an unfurled scroll. "As you say."

"Do you know how the Kaito family daimyō is chosen?"

She shook her head.

"Among the artifacts of Cliffside Shrine is a catalpa bow that once belonged to our family's founder. Named Mikazuki, it is said to be the home of an awakened kami, one that so adored High Priestess Kaito that it recognizes her children. Only the true family daimyō can string Mikazuki. For anyone else, the bow resists, and the string breaks." He regarded her sideways. "Of course, in order to discover you are the daimyō, you must be willing to try."

Her eyes widened. "Isawa Kaito's yumi chooses the Kaito daimyō?"

"There is no choosing. Mikazuki recognizes its wielder. I watched my relatives try, women and men I felt were far more worthy than I. Had I not attempted to string it, I would have never known Mikazuki was meant for me."

She remembered Ofushikai as it was placed in her hands, the sword unsheathing on its own, her breath caught among a sea of gasps.

"Part-way up the mountain is a waterfall. I have often found it refreshing after a night of difficult sleep. Helps me to rebalance." He looked at her. "I will tell you where it is, just in case."

From beyond the garden came the sound of a bell, followed by cheers and shouts. "The midday offering," he explained. But from his furrowed brow, Tsukune could tell something was not right.

She followed him to the monastery square. There, a noisy crowd had gathered around a pear tree. At the center, Uwazuru was stringing his bow.

"It seems someone has challenged my son," said Nobukai.

"What is this?" Tsukune asked.

"An archery display to please the kami. Some use it as an opportunity to compete." He cast her a glance. "I realize some may disapprove." Many in the Isawa considered such displays to be ostentatious and disrespectful.

"Competition is healthy," she replied. "We did it all the time in the dōjō."

She caught his slight smile, though he tried to hide it.

The crowd quieted as the challenger stepped forward. Tsukune recognized her bobbing ponytail and the birthmark across her eye. Kosori tugged on her three-fingered glove and bowed to her cousin.

"They used to do this as children," Nobukai admitted, stroking his chin. "But I thought they had grown out of it. Why the renewed rivalry, I wonder?"

Tsukune blanched. Was this because she had complimented Kosori's archery?

Kosori pointed to a pear on a branch and nocked her arrow. She made an effortless release, and it fell to the ground. Polite clapping filled the square.

"Now Uwazuru must make the same shot," Nobukai explained.

"Like in the Bowman's Wager."

Nobukai straightened. "Our family had a hand in the creation of that tradition."

Tsukune concealed a smirk. Her own sensei had once claimed the same thing.

After Uwazuru made the same shot and received the same

applause, a woman waded into the crowd carrying a primitive helmet of soot-colored iron bands. Angry exclamations rose from the crowd, and someone threw a pear at it. "A Yobanjin lost this helmet!" the woman cried. "Here, Uwazuru! Show us how to properly treat it!"

Grinning, Uwazuru pointed his bow, drawing slowly. Tsukune could not comprehend his strategy. It was not a difficult target. But then he turned his wrists in opposite directions, twisting the string. He released, and the arrow smashed through the iron, the mangled tip emerging from the back. The crowd exploded with applause. Tsukune's jaw slackened. "How?"

"Twisting the draw," Nobukai said, demonstrating the movement with his hands. "In this way, one increases the tension in the string beyond what is normal. It increases power at the cost of accuracy. Or it would," he added, "if one did not have the kami to guide the arrow."

The crowd hushed. Kosori set her arrow. Even at this vantage, Tsukune saw her tremble.

"Yet it is not that easy," he continued. "The yumi is delicate. It will break if mishandled or pulled too hard. Instead, one must be gentle. Humble. One cannot command. One must ask."

Kosori released. The arrow broke through. Kosori blinked at her accomplishment, as if she could not quite believe it. As the crowd applauded, Kosori flashed Uwazuru a triumphant smile.

"There," said Nobukai. "She just made her mistake."

"Does someone have a coin?" Kosori called out.

"Here!" Someone pushed their way forward, offering a string of copper disks, each with a diamond-shaped hole punched from the center.

"Toss it up," Kosori said, loading her bow.

A pit formed in Tsukune's stomach. Even so, as the coin was flipped, somersaulting vertically above the crowd, she inhaled in tandem with Kosori's draw, hope filling her chest. *She'll land it,* Tsukune thought. *She wouldn't call the shot if she—*

The arrow slipped. The coin bounced on the ground, untouched.

Kosori's face turned the crimson shade of a mountain peach. Blanching, Tsukune felt as if she had been the one to pull the string herself.

"Let's try again," said Uwazuru. The crowd recovered the disk.

He drew as it was tossed again, then released. A clear note rang, the coin spinning as the arrow struck it.

Beneath the cheers and Uwazuru's chanted name, Kosori's head sank. She turned suddenly, and her eyes locked with Tsukune's. Her face blanched. She spun away, but not before Tsukune caught her horrified expression. Nobukai said something, but his voice faded into the background as Tsukune gaped in dread at the unwitting role she had played in Kosori's humiliation.

"Shiba Tsukune-sama! I hope you are enjoying your afternoon!"

Tsukune paused, awkward and off guard, her bathing tunic folded under her arm. The old man from the previous day's court smiled at her from his seat on the rocks. The roar of the crashing waterfall behind him drowned out the bush warblers and mountain bugs.

She gave a stiff bow, tugging her kimono collar tighter. "Asako Maezawa-sama. Forgive my interruption, I didn't realize—"

"Bah!" The old man swatted the air. "I just finished. You will soon have it to yourself." He gestured to the top of the roaring waterfall. "These days, nothing else banishes the aches. Did you know these cascades were frozen until only a century ago?"

She shook her head and placed her bathing tunic on a flat stone, blinking in the spray. In his gentle and wrinkled smile, she dimly recalled her grandfather.

He gestured for her to join him at the water's edge. "How have you found the Kaito so far?"

"A little strange," she admitted, "but I am growing fond of them."

"Is that so?"

She cupped her hands. Icy water stung her palms. "At first I found their affinity for archery odd, but I'm starting to understand that they don't regard *kyūjutsu* as a purely martial practice. And they have an unabashed way about them that I find charming."

"When you've known them as long as I have, you come to adore their open innocence. The frog in the well knows nothing of the ocean, as the saying goes."

"You must have served them for some time."

"Oh, no. While I have history with the Kaito, my being here now is a recent development." He fished his pipe from his sleeve. "I serve on behalf of the Asako daimyō. My function is to advise Lord

Nobukai on matters regarding Cliffside Shrine."

"The shrine?" Tsukune straightened. "Why would the Kaito require advice for their own shrine?"

Maezawa lit his pipe. "You've been there. Have you not noticed anything awry?"

She watched their wavering reflections for a time, then sat beside him. Their voices would not carry beyond the crashing waterfall. "I have," she admitted. "But I wasn't sure if I was imagining things."

"You are not," he replied. He seemed to be deciding something. "I understand you were trained among the Lion Clan?"

"Yes. The Akodo War College. I studied there for years, until…"

Even so far from home, even before the black-ribboned letter had come, she'd felt it. Like autumn leaves, she'd felt her soul grow lighter. That was how she'd known her brother was gone.

Her voice faltered, her throat closing. After all this time, she still couldn't speak of it.

"But after, you returned to the Shiba Guardian School."

She nodded.

Maezawa sat back and puffed as Tsukune waited. "So," he finally spoke again, "the yōjimbō training, it makes one observant, yes? Always watching for dangers? And as protectors of the Isawa, one also learns something of the kami?"

"These things are true," she said.

"So then, what have you noticed about Cliffside Shrine?"

She closed her eyes. She could see every crack in the ancient wood, hear the rattling of the brittle streamers, smell the rot and stale dust. "The shimenawa. They are fraying. I spoke with Nobukai about them today. He said the blessing ropes were simply aging."

"Blessing ropes, you say?"

"That is what he called them."

His knowing eyes twinkled. "But you know better, yes?"

She nodded darkly. "He thought I could not tell the difference. But we learn such things as yōjimbō to shugenja. They were ropes of *binding*. They make the walls not of houses, but of prisons."

"Very good," said Maezawa. "He underestimated you."

"There is something else," she continued. "I heard whispers."

His eyebrows climbed his wrinkled forehead. "Whispers? What did they say?"

"I'm not sure," she confessed. "I heard them once coming from the inner shrine, and before that, I heard them while climbing up the mountain."

His smile faltered for only a moment. "From all this, what might one conclude?"

"Kosori-san told me Isawa Kaito gave her life to seal away a demon. The Kaito's duty is to protect this shrine, which contains ropes of binding. There is nothing natural about the decay," she concluded. "Something is trying to escape the shrine."

"Astute." Maezawa tapped the bowl of his pipe. As he did, Tsukune thought she caught a glimpse of something etched on his palm, a black tattoo of some kind, perhaps an eye. But in the next moment it was obscured, and Tsukune could not confirm what she'd seen.

"Surely the Kaito realize this?" she asked.

"Some may suspect something is amiss, but they have chosen to say nothing of it."

Tsukune stood. "If they know, they should say something! To me! To the council!"

"And lose face in the clan?" Maezawa was smiling, but regarded her as one might a child. "Try to understand, Tsukune-sama. These people have lived in the mountains all their lives. It is not like the city, where resources are plentiful. The world has taught them self-reliance, to shoulder their burdens alone. To reveal their trouble would be to admit they cannot perform their duty. It is unthinkable for such a small family. So, they endure and carry on."

Tsukune frowned in spite of her understanding.

"In any case," Maezawa continued, "the council already knows. Do you not think it strange that the Masters would take interest in one student's death?" His voice lowered. "The truth is, people have been vanishing around that shrine for months now. At least eight have perished so far. Servants at first, then Kaito, then the student..."

The waterfall's spray grew suddenly colder. One was bad enough, a poor student with a lifetime before her, a door closed too soon. But eight? Eight souls lost for the Kaito's pride? Her kin. Her people. Gone. Tsukune's fist clenched. Unacceptable. "Then Tadaka is merely confirming the council's suspicions," she said coldly.

"If only Nobukai would admit the problem, perhaps a disaster could be averted. I have advised him to do so for some time. But Tadaka's presence has caused Nobukai to hesitate, and the shrine's decay accelerated after his arrival. I fear he is inadvertently making things worse."

Tsukune shook her head. "That is not possible. Tadaka is a shugenja. His world and that of the kami are one."

"There is a darkness within him, Tsukune-sama. You have seen it yourself."

And she had seen it, just the other night. His stony look on the balcony, drinking the light, the way he'd just brushed her aside… Was this why the council had rejected his proposal?

She spoke carefully. "If I were to convince Tadaka to leave with me tonight and make his report, do you think you could make Nobukai see the wisdom of approaching the Masters?"

"Do you think you could do this?"

She looked at her uncertain reflection. When they were together, he'd made the decisions for them both. As a mere bodyguard, it was not a yōjimbō's place to say otherwise.

"I am not sure," she confessed. "The Shiba serve the Isawa, not the other way around."

Maezawa leaned back, looking her up and down. "My eyes play tricks. All this time, I thought you were the Phoenix Champion! If you were, you'd be sworn to protect the Isawa, and acting on behalf of the Kaito would be your duty."

She bit her lip. Things were not the same between them since she'd taken up Ofushikai. She had risen, while he had fallen from favor. He was colder now. The longer he stayed here, the darker his shadow would become. But if she did this, if she manipulated him or took charge, surely Tadaka would resent her forever.

Could she live with that? Knowing that the one person who had been there in her time of loss, the one who had given her purpose, who could set her blood aflame, wanted nothing more to do with her? Wetness bubbled up in her eyes. What could be worse than losing him for that?

Losing him to the darkness. To whatever the shrine imprisoned. That would be worse. Especially if she could have saved him.

Tsukune swallowed the knot in her throat and nodded. "I will do my best."

There was no time for *misogi* now. She turned to leave, casting Maezawa one final look. He was watching the waters, silent. Her heart churned with a final question. "Do you think the council will judge the Kaito harshly?" She recalled Kosori's guileless smile. *All of them?*

The back of his head rose. "We all have our roles to play, Tsukune-sama. The Asako heal, the Shiba protect, and the Isawa... *know.*"

She did not understand. But perhaps she didn't need to.

Chapter Five

Tsukune nearly tumbled into Kosori as she rounded the corner. The girl was waiting outside her quarters, and she immediately doubled over in a steep bow. "I have come to beg mercy for my family."

Tsukune blinked, eyes wide. *What?* Before she could utter a bewildered word, Kosori dropped, palms up: a submissive gesture as old as the Empire. "How can I demonstrate my sincerity?"

Tsukune rolled open her door. "Not out here."

Kosori plopped herself down at the center of Tsukune's room and fidgeted with her prayer beads. Tsukune closed the door and rubbed her forehead. She didn't have time for this. She had to find Tadaka, convince him to leave with her, and…

And what? For that matter, how? The thought of pulling rank, of commanding him like a mere vassal, froze her blood. She could never do that. Why should he listen to his former yōjimbō when he would not even heed the word of his own sensei, an Elemental Master?

Kosori was staring. Tsukune looked to her window. How could she face the trusting girl now, with what she was about to do? But it surely had taken Kosori great courage to come like this, a mere samurai compared to Tsukune's rank as daimyō, risking a breach of etiquette. With all Kosori had done for her, was she not obligated to hear the girl out? Tsukune inwardly grimaced. What would Tetsu say, if he were here?

One opponent at a time, Tsukune-sama. No matter how large or sudden, that is how you defeat an ambush.

He was right, of course. She breathed slowly until the muscles in her neck relaxed. Finally, she spoke. "What did you mean just now?"

Kosori made a wry face. "I'm just the girl who cleans the shrine. I'm only good for pushing dust. But I am not daft. First came Maezawa, then a council representative. And now you, the Phoenix Clan Champion." Her fists tightened. "You came to decide my family's fate."

"You're mistaken," she whispered.

Confusion flickered across Kosori's features. "But…then why keep your identity secret? Why try to enter the inner shrine?"

Her face went hot. "I heard voices," she said. "As for my identity… well…"

"Voices?" The alarm in Kosori's voice, her pale face.

Tsukune's haragei spun. She sat before her. "Kosori, you must trust me. How long have you known the shrine's wards are failing?"

"Almost a year now." Shame pulled her gaze to the floor. "My *shufuku* was ten months ago." When Tsukune looked confused, she clarified, "My coming-of-age."

The regional dialect. "Your gempuku," Tsukune corrected.

"Due to my…underperformance…I was assigned to the shrine's upkeep. Cleaning and scrubbing every day, how could I not notice the ropes decaying? I knew something was wrong. But they didn't believe me! Whenever I brought it up, they said I was desperate for promotion, or trying to escape my duties." She leaned forward. "It's true that I felt my lot was unfair, but I wouldn't lie about something so grave!"

"Did you ever approach your uncle about this?"

Kosori blanched. "So you know." She hesitated. "Yes. He forbade me to speak of it."

"Why?"

"I'm not sure. At first I thought it was because he didn't believe me. But he's been visiting the shrine at night, reconsecrating, replacing blessed streamers, applying new wards. Still, this is not enough to keep it from escaping."

Tsukune's eyes narrowed. "The demon, you mean."

"That is one way to read the word. We pronounce it *ateru*. It's a kind of malicious spirit."

Tsukune produced paper and charcoal from her desk. "Show me."

She did not recognize the kanji Kosori drew, although it almost looked like the word for "blame." It was a rural word, a product of the regional dialect.

Kosori continued, "Isawa Kaito bound the ateru to a well in exchange for her life. The shrine was built to contain it. I don't know why the wards are failing now."

Tsukune's head reeled. "Are you telling me that your uncle knowingly kept the failing wards a secret from the Isawa, and instead sought to repair them himself?"

"He tried to preserve face while addressing the danger as best he could."

"Kosori," Tsukune said. "Eight people are dead."

The evening birdsongs drew the sun below the horizon, lighting it aflame. Kosori shook in the amber light, struggling to maintain some dignity. Tsukune felt sorry for her. However, there was no denying that Nobukai had shown poor judgment in the execution of his duties. He had shamed his family and the Phoenix.

And the Kaito would be punished. All of them. Kosori's beads clacked as she fidgeted, her head stooped low. Just yesterday, in the shrine, their positions had been exchanged.

They need you, Tsukune.

Against the wall, on its stand, Ofushikai glowed in the twilight.

"All right," she said. "I think I can help things."

Kosori lifted her head.

"I believe the Kaito are not wholly responsible for these events. I am prepared to testify to this in defense of your family. However, Kosori-san, it will mean little if your uncle does not accept the blame and demonstrate his remorse. If you wish to do him any favors, you will convince him to approach the Council of Elemental Masters on his knees and ask for help. They may show lenience."

Kosori nodded eagerly. "I…I can never repay you." She bowed. "Thank you, Shiba-ue."

Tsukune winced. "Don't. Others may call me that, but for you, it is 'Tsukune-san.'" She offered a smile. "We're friends, aren't we?"

Kosori's eyes glimmered with a faint wet sheen. She sniffled and nodded.

Tsukune rose, donning her silk jacket. "Now I must find Tadaka."

"He's at the shrine," Kosori said, recomposing herself. "I passed him on my way here."

"Then I must go there and—"

She paused. And what, exactly? Somehow convince him to deliver a report that was sympathetic to the Kaito and laid the blame solely at their daimyō's feet? A man who had offered her sympathy, a man she'd promised to help?

Chase two hares, and you won't catch either.

She nodded. "Yes. One thing at a time. First, I find Tadaka. The rest will follow."

If Kosori wondered with whom Tsukune was speaking, she did not say so.

Tsukune hesitated by the door, then at the last moment, took Ofushikai from the stand. She tucked the sword between her obi's first and second layers, turning it so the edge faced downward, as suited blades predating the katana. Then she tucked in her *wakizashi* vertically.

Kosori stared at the ancient blade with wonder. "Is that—?"

"I do not plan to use it," Tsukune assured her. "I will need to look authoritative. Tadaka is…stoic."

"That is a polite way to say it," Kosori replied.

Two armed men passed Tsukune and Kosori on the dusky streets, sparing them not even a glance. When they were gone, Tsukune questioned Kosori with a look. "The guards of Cliffside Shrine," Kosori replied. "If I were to guess, I'd say they are reporting to Uncle."

Tsukune quickened her steps.

They found Tadaka partway across the swinging bridge, the last of the sun's rays tracing his outline. She called out, and he paused, waiting, face impassive beneath his cone-shaped hat.

"Good evening, Tsukune-sama," he said, his tone all business. "Out for an evening walk?" He glanced at Kosori. "And you brought your friend."

"What are you doing?" she blurted.

"I have a theory about the shrine pertaining to my investigation, but I must test it after dark." He resumed his steady walk. "Not that it concerns you."

"I know what's going on," she said, keeping stride with effort. "The other deaths, the decaying wards…"

"You know all of that, do you?"

"Listen. I know you think—" She stopped. There were whispers, layered and faint, but clear. She looked down into the ravine, where the jagged earth was parted, the gap seeming no wider than the space between two closed shōji doors…

"Tsukune?"

The whispers vanished. Even in his annoyed state, Tadaka's concern was clear.

She looked into his shadowy face. *There is a darkness inside him.*

"There are horses at the closest village," she said. "We can be at Kyūden Isawa within days. You have enough to give your report. We can deliver it together."

He shook his head. "Deliver yours, if you have one to give. Mine is not yet done." He gestured ahead, where dim light flickered behind the massive shrine's paper walls. "These events are not random circumstance. There is something even more sinister afoot, something that could affect all of the Phoenix lands. And I intend to prove it."

"What are you talking about?" said Kosori.

Tsukune cringed. "Let me handle this," she told the girl as Kosori glared. She met Tadaka's eyes. "What do you believe you have found?"

Tadaka searched her face in the fading light. For a moment, his look was the same as when they had been together all those months ago. Then, he turned away. "Nothing for either of you. Go back. I must do this alone."

Tsukune looked at her hands. She'd been a fool to think she could reason with him. He wouldn't listen to her. He didn't take her seriously.

Did anyone? In that moment, she saw Tetsu's disappointed face. The way he stared at her sword. Like she didn't deserve it. Like she wasn't strong enough. Just a yōjimbō. Nothing more.

She gritted her teeth. Ofushikai had chosen her. She was Phoenix Clan Champion. Now, what was she going to do about it?

In three steps, she had tangled her fingers in his sleeve and balled her fist, pulling, forcing him to look at her. His annoyed expression melted into one of surprise. He tried to pull away, but she held him fast.

"This is the part of the Kabuki play I cannot stand, when the wise sage *could* tell the samurai what is about to happen, but chooses not to. It is the worst part of the play, don't you think?"

He frowned. "Perhaps he seeks to protect the samurai from things she doesn't understand."

"That is for me to decide, not you." Her heart raced, but she cast this aside, matching his eyes and not shrinking away. "I may not be your yōjimbō anymore, Tadaka-san, but I am your clan champion." *Even if we are no longer friends.* "If you have found something, then you will show me."

They stood there, opposed, like the sun and moon.

"Fine," he said and freed himself. Wordless, he continued across.

Tsukune exhaled a tiny cloud.

"So," Kosori softly remarked, "you were just his yōjimbō?"

"Perhaps it was more complex than that," Tsukune admitted. Her heart was still racing, but it was exhilaration that pumped hot blood through her limbs now. She wasn't sure where her outburst had come from, but it felt good.

"Why are you following him? He doesn't want your help."

Tsukune looked out over the mountains set against the fading sky. She had no answer for that. "Once he finds what he needs, I will escort him back to the council. That is my duty, as is the protection of the Isawa." She glanced at Kosori. "That includes you, you know. You can go back if you wish. I do not want you to get in trouble with your uncle."

"Uncle is in more trouble than I." She made a stern face. "I deserve to know what Tadaka thinks he has found. Besides," she added, "I'd like to see his face if he's wrong."

"So would I," Tsukune agreed. Although, she inwardly admitted, he rarely was.

The shrine at night retained little of its welcoming presence. Stone lanterns smoked with the cabbage-like scent of rapeseed oil, their glow not reaching far. The moon painted the shrine in pale tones and left corners dark. The paper streamers waved lazily from the rafters, giving the impression of spider silk. Tsukune's gaze was reflexively drawn to every twitching shadow, and she habitually positioned herself between the shadows and the others, her hand constantly flinching for her sword and then relaxing.

"Leave that sheathed," Tadaka advised. "A shrine is no place for a sword."

Tsukune swallowed her retort, that a shrine is where she had received the sword. She'd brought Ofushikai on impulse. Looking back on it now, she wondered why.

They stalked the shrine's rooms, Tadaka's beads swinging from his limp hand. Now and again he would stop and tilt his head. Tsukune strained to listen, but no whispers came—only the wind and her own shaking breath.

Tadaka took a shimenawa and examined where it had frayed, then the paper tag affixed to it. "Did you make these?" he asked Kosori. She nodded. "You have some talent. Were the presence in this shrine weaker, these tags might have been adequate." He squinted at the tear, then held out the rope for the others to see. "Does this seem like the rope is unwinding itself from age, or does it appear as if it were being cut?"

"I'm sure I can't say," Kosori replied, but the jagged sawtooth pattern left no doubt in Tsukune's mind. She and Tadaka shared a knowing glance before he left the rope swinging.

Entering the southwestern room, Tsukune choked on dust. The moonlight through the open box-shaped skylight glinted off dust motes, and more white tags nearly glowed on their fraying ropes. The light flickered, and through the open skylight, a swarm of moths fluttered past, casting a single sprawling shadow. Tsukune nearly drew Ofushikai, then slowly relaxed.

The hairs on her neck were still standing when they entered the central chamber. Tadaka shook his head grimly. "Kosori-san, the presence in this shrine is very active. How could you have let things degenerate so far?"

Kosori's jaw clenched, and a crimson tint touched her cheeks.

"Leave her be," Tsukune said. "She did what she could."

Tadaka scoffed. "Did she, now? A few wards for the ropes? Scrubbing the floor?"

"She alerted the council." Tsukune smiled at her. "She is Hototogisu."

Kosori's mouth fell agape. "H-how did you know?"

"It was your childhood name. Your uncle told me."

Tadaka looked to Kosori with new eyes. "Ah, so you wrote that letter. I misjudged you, Kosori-san. My apologies."

Tsukune rolled her eyes. *And I have misjudged you as well, Tsukune-san. What a clever deduction!*

"You've learned what you need, then?" Kosori said. "We're done?"

Tadaka regarded the closed screen depicting Isawa Kaito. "Not quite," he replied and stepped onto the stage.

Kosori looked horrified. "You're going into the inner sanctum?"

"It is the one place I have not yet investigated." He whispered apologies as he placed a hand on the screen. Tsukune's heart thundered in her ears. She held her breath and braced for a crashing wave. He slid it open. Beyond, the world abruptly ended in void.

"Bring a candle," he said.

Kosori obeyed, procuring two from nearby and lighting them with the lanterns. She hoisted herself onto the stage and surrendered a candle to the much taller man. Beyond the screen, the light revealed a deeper chamber and another set of doors. Tsukune felt like a taut bow, pulled in two directions. Tadaka knew she wouldn't follow. He strode beyond in a bubble of light. Kosori hesitantly went, leaving Tsukune behind.

Go, Tsukune! Now! Go!

The unbidden voice filled her limbs with urgent energy. She felt that she was standing before a closing door, and once it shut, she would never see the other side. She leapt onto the stage and passed the screen, not stopping until she was at the second set of doors.

In the wake of the shattered taboo, she looked up into Tadaka's surprised face and slowly smiled. *That's right,* she thought. *There's more to me than you believed, isn't there?* She was ready to counter any argument, but he offered none. Kosori exhaled with visible relief. "Behind me," Tsukune said, and slid the door aside.

The inner sanctum was vaster than she had anticipated, the polished floors and plain walls stretching well beyond the candle's reach. Dozens of paper wards lay flat against the ceiling. Silk lanterns, pale orbs on strings, hung in rows. An oil trough lined the walls, the spicy scent of cassia anointing oil ever-present. A row of dollhouses served as the shrines to the Kaito's honored ancestors.

"Is this the only interior room?" Tadaka asked, striding inside without hesitation.

Kosori timidly gestured into the dark. "The offering hall is that way. There are some rooms farther in the back. I'm normally not allowed in here," she added, casting Tsukune a meaningful look.

As Tadaka methodically stalked the chamber, Tsukune followed Kosori on a winding path. Small artifacts lay in designated spaces throughout the room. They paused by a shelf where an unstrung yumi was enshrined on a bow stand. It was ancient and tall, wrapped in rattan and adorned with silk tassels and a glittering bell. Kosori gasped when she saw it.

"Mikazuki," she breathed. "That's the bow of Kaito herself."

Other than the adornments, it looked like any other bow, if very old. "Have you ever seen it before now?" Tsukune asked.

"Only once," Kosori replied. She dipped her head reverently. "It only leaves the shrine when it is time to determine the new daimyō."

This is your family's Ofushikai, Tsukune thought.

Beneath was a small offerings bowl. Tsukune reached into her pouch and withdrew a spindle of incense, which she placed inside.

"You keep incense?" Kosori asked as Tsukune skillfully lit it with the candle.

"Of course. Every Shiba does. It's a long tradition." She inhaled the thin smoke. Aloeswood, cinnamon, and ginger lily. "Before a battle, it is customary to burn incense in one's helmet. That way, if your opponent takes your head, at least it will smell nice."

Tadaka grunted. At the center of the chamber was a short stone well. Shimenawa decorated its circumference, while a slanted roof sheltered the opening. "So this is where Isawa Kaito bound the demon." Inside, Tadaka's candle glinted off untroubled waters.

Kosori gawked into the portal. "That's...not right," she muttered. "It should be frozen. The stories said..."

Tadaka's eyes fell to the back of the room, where his candle revealed an altar with a lidless lacquered box. His prayer beads were like a windswept porch swing. "Found it," he said.

Whispers. All at once, thundering. Tsukune could barely hear her own thoughts over the sudden layered voices.

Inside the box lay a dagger. Golden light thinly coated the splotchy ancient metal of the curved blade. Its handle was twice its length and appeared to be carved from bone. The voices stroked Tsukune's aching mind. Her fingers extended, reaching...

Don't!

She jerked back. The whispers stopped. Slowly she uncurled her fingers from the handle of Ofushikai, not recalling when she'd grabbed it.

Tadaka stuck the candle on a stand by the altar and wove his prayer beads around the fingers of his right hand. Although he looked grim, his eyes were victorious. "This may be the proof," he said. "I must bring this to the Masters."

"No!" Kosori's protest bounced through the chamber. "I can't let you take artifacts from the shrine!"

Tadaka spun. "Then you admit this is a Kaito family artifact?"

"Enough, Tadaka." Tsukune moved between them. "What is it?"

"I must study it to be certain," he said. "However, if I am correct, this dagger suggests the presence trapped here is not merely trying to escape. It is being aided." Tadaka glared at Kosori. "By your uncle."

Amber light filled Kosori's wide eyes. "That's not true." She met Tsukune's horrified stare. "It's not true!"

Tadaka continued. "I must investigate further, but daggers of such design dating from the fifth century were commonly used for blood offerings." He made a protective gesture. "If there truly is a demon sealed within this temple, then it is a denizen of Jigoku."

Only Tadaka would be so bold as to speak the name aloud. Jigoku was the Realm of Evil, the source of all corruption and the Shadowlands Taint. It was a labyrinthine maelstrom of pain and suffering, with rivers of blood, mountains of bone, and countless horrors.

Of course. That was why Tadaka would not let this go. If his Shadowlands knowledge exposed the Kaito daimyō's misdeeds, then the Masters could never deny the validity of his research. They would have to accept his proposal.

And if he went, he would never come back. *There is a darkness inside him.* He'd be lost to her forever.

"You are mistaken!" Kosori trembled, her fists balled. "My uncle may have made mistakes, but he is not a *mahō-tsukai!*"

Tsukune winced at the word. Witch.

Anger flickered across Tadaka's features. "Oh, no? You believe the wards were ruined on their own?" He jutted a finger. "He hid a demon's awakening. To what end?"

"You could never understand! Without the shrine, the Kaito are nothing!"

Tadaka was stone-faced. "Perhaps the deaths were sacrifices."

Kosori hissed through clenched teeth. "Take. That. Back."

Now was no time for this. Tsukune opened her mouth. A sudden burst of pain popped behind her eyes, rattling her teeth. The floor seemed to warp beneath her feet. She staggered.

The weight of Tadaka's hand on her shoulder brought her back. "What is it?" His posturing was gone, only his concern remaining. "Breathe slowly, Tsukune."

She hadn't realized she was drawing rapid breaths. "I just need a moment."

"What is the meaning of this?"

Kaito no Isawa Nobukai stood at the door, wearing brocaded robes and an outraged expression. He was flanked by shrine keepers, paper lanterns, and bows. They unfurled to either side of him. The last to enter was tapping a pipe with a knotted hand, his old eyes looking disappointed to see the three youngsters within.

Tsukune spoke his name. "Asako Maezawa."

The old man sighed at Tadaka. "Disregarding the champion's advice? I did not think even you were so stubborn." It was the first time Tsukune had seen him without a smile.

Nobukai's eyes flashed at his niece. "You let outsiders into the inner sanctum?" He stepped forward. "You must leave at once! All of you!"

"I am afraid that is impossible," Tadaka replied. "I have seen the dagger. You realize how this looks."

"It is not what you think! Come outside and I will explain."

"What is going on?" Tsukune demanded of Maezawa. Her hand twitched.

"Don't act rashly," he advised. "Violence in the shrine is unbecoming."

Her eyes narrowed. "Whose side are you on, exactly?"

"The Phoenix's," Maezawa replied.

"You are interrupting a ritual!" Nobukai said, his voice tinged with desperation. "If you do not leave—"

A flame floated at the center of the room, radiating a glowing violet light. It had not been there just before. Kosori looked as though she were staring into a dragon's maw.

"No!" cried Nobukai. "Not them! I beg you!" He fell to his knees. "This was not our deal!"

"Deal?" Tadaka thundered. "What deals have you made with this demon, Nobukai?"

Tsukune tensed. If the Kaito daimyō had made a pact with a demon, she would have to take his life, right here, right now.

The daimyō spoke with a defeated voice. "This was an appeasement ritual," he said. "You have just been mistaken for the offering."

A breeze stirred the hanging lanterns. They began to glow, a sickly pale glowworm purple. The flame expanded, assuming a vaguely humanoid form. Sweat dotted Tsukune's brow. It was becoming like a furnace.

"The wards will hold him," Nobukai shouted. "But you must leave now!"

Kosori's eyes glittered. "Uncle? Were the deaths really sacrifices to appease the ateru?"

Nobukai paled. "Who told you that? You cannot possibly believe such a thing!"

"I don't know what to believe. I thought you were trying to save our family's face and contain the ateru. But now I see you're trying to free it!"

"He is freeing himself!" Nobukai protested. "When the well thawed, he—" The daimyō gasped. His arms fell limply. "Now it is too late."

A resounding pop, and the flames peeled away. It was an emaciated human, translucent and floating. Its black hair and long mustache whipped violently around its head, as if trapped in invisible winds, but the triangular cloth tied to its forehead remained serene. Beneath a tattered white tunic of a style Tsukune did not recognize, its legs faded away at the ankles. A black flame was etched onto the creature's face. When it opened its eyes, the whites burned like fire, and a torrent of layered whispers thundered in Tsukune's ears.

"An *onryō*?" Tadaka thrust out his hand. "*That's* your demon? A vengeful ghost? The so-called 'ateru' is nothing more than a—"

He deflated, broad shoulders slumping, his mirthless voice dropping in volume. "Of course. What else could it have been?" As it was unrelated to Jigoku, defeating it would prove nothing to the council. There would never be a chance to convince them to support his proposal.

She would have felt sorry for him if her yōjimbō instincts weren't roaring, turning her stomach into an oxcart wheel. The apparition's smile spread beyond its face's boundaries, splitting its head in two. "Tadaka!" she urged. "Stay behind me."

The shrine keepers were stringing bows. Nobukai drew a paper ward from his obi. "Begone, demon! Return whence you came!"

"No," Tadaka spoke, his moment of self-pity falling away. "You had your chance." He drew a scroll, working off the bindings. "Now a representative of the council will handle this for good." He unfurled the paper and read, his voice like an echoing bell.

Tsukune looked from face to face. Nobukai held his breath. Kosori stared limply. They were almost hopeful. It was Maezawa's expression that made her heart quail. His knowing frown. His stoic resolution. Whatever Tadaka was attempting, the old man knew it would not work. And if that was so…

Its mouth parted. A thousand needles glinted in the light. It rushed forward, blurring, its elongated fingers rending the air as it issued a spectral scream.

No thought preceded action. Tsukune had drilled in this a thousand times. She stepped in the way of the creature's strike, shoving Tadaka behind her. Ofushikai sang a brilliant note as she freed it. She cleaved the ghost in half. It vanished like smoke.

Only after she'd remained in her attack stance for long moments did she return to a defensive posture, finally noticing the open horror on the faces of the others. She froze under their gaze, her mind catching up to her actions.

Tadaka seized her before she could reply, affixing her with stony eyes. "You drew the sword," he uttered. "In this blessed chamber, you drew steel." He stared up at the ceiling. "It is no longer sanctified."

As cold realization washed over her, the wards on the ceiling came away, falling gently like flakes of snow.

Chapter Six

For a long time, no one moved. They searched the gloom beyond their impotent lanterns. Tsukune could not tell if she saw movement, or if these were merely tricks played by her straining eyes. There came a muted rumble from outside, followed by the drumming of wet fingers on the roof. A storm had broken, an oppressive blanket further dimming all senses.

Perhaps she'd banished it after all. Tsukune swallowed and moved in front of Tadaka. No. If she had, then surely the unnatural viridian glow of the shrine's lanterns would have been extinguished, and Nobukai's face would not be so pale in the gloom.

Slowly, one of the shrine keepers began stringing their bow— *the pluck of a bowstring could banish spirits.* Having tied one end, he bent the yumi against the floor to string the other. It fought him, but he wrestled it into place, then gingerly grasped for the loop.

A screaming face bolted toward them from the dark.

The shrine keeper flinched. The bow slipped. There was a whip-crack sound, followed by a wet thud. In the dim lantern light, the bow limb protruded from his impaled, lifeless body.

The face vanished, its hot laughter echoing throughout the room.

She couldn't think. She couldn't move. She just stared at the dark pool slowly expanding.

The keepers dropped their bows and drew wands with paper streamers. They encircled Nobukai. Kosori, although unarmed, fell into their ranks.

A dark blur lashed out, swallowing up another keeper. His scream was abruptly silenced, followed by a hot splash. Tsukune vividly imagined a gutted fish.

She pressed her back into Tadaka's. He had drawn an agarwood rod and held it protectively. "It's toying with us," he told her. "It will pick us off, one by one."

"Can you do anything?" she asked.

"I'll need time," he replied.

Nobukai's voice rose above the din. "The anointing oil! Light it! Then it cannot hide!"

Kosori darted out, scooping up a dropped lantern. A sudden movement speared out from the dark, but another keeper threw themself in the path and was wetly engulfed. Kosori spun and let go. The paper orb smashed into the stone trough. Flames spread quickly, tearing away the curtains of darkness. Tsukune readied her sword. She would throw herself at the ghost with all her power.

A wall of wooden faces stared back.

There were dozens, elongated and thin, their burial clothing splotchy and torn. They filled every corner, clinging to the walls like spiders. The eyes behind their burial masks were hateful coals. Among them, hands red and glistening, the ateru smiled.

The spectral wave crashed upon them. Tsukune lost herself in a sea of claws and screaming faces, the only light Ofushikai's flashing steel as it cleaved ethereal bodies, each cut shearing a ghost and leaving tendrils of fog. Hot blood splashed on her face. She didn't think. She just cut.

Then, Tadaka's rhythmic chanting rose above the mass. At the center of the violent storm, he held out his fragrant agarwood, and the ghosts broke around him like a diverging river. Tsukune cut her way toward him, deflecting, slicing. Every exertion slowed her a little more. In each brief pause between opponents, she saw no fewer of them.

So this is why warriors prefer duels, she thought. *They are over instantly, while battles seem never ending.*

The Kaito fought valiantly, but with the grim resolution of inevitable death. There were too many ghosts. Nobukai darted from his dwindling circle to the bow stand where Mikazuki rested. It nearly scraped the ceiling as he pulled it free. With a wrist flick his bowstring was in his hands. The bow seemed to curve on its own at his touch.

A flash of light. Nobukai fell. The ancient bow clattered to the ground. A few moments later, so did his arm.

They leapt upon him. Tearing. Biting. Screaming. They drew red trails across his body. One reared back with animal eyes, reeling for the death strike.

"Don't touch him!" Kosori screamed. Clutched in her hands was a broom. She barreled into them, swiping with broad strokes. They recoiled, as if she were waving a torch. They formed a circle around her and her ruined uncle, stepping back when she threatened them with the broom, encroaching again when she swept at another.

Incredible. "How is that working?" Tsukune called out.

Tadaka's eyes looked urgently behind her. She turned, too late, toward the specter that was leaping, bony fingers reaching out toward her throat. There was no time to deflect or duck or do anything but numbly watch her own death. In that fossilized moment, she prayed that she would die on her face and not disgracefully on her back.

The strike never came. The ghost crashed into plated armor licked with white flames, impaled by a spear of radiant light. The crest of the Phoenix was a beacon on the newcomer's back. The armored warrior drew an ethereal blade and severed the ghost's head with a deft strike. The ghost burned up in heatless flames, ashes floating to brush Tsukune's cheek.

She recognized the newcomer's armor and knew the fighting style. She had seen them both in his student Tetsu. Her rescuer's name came to her lips. "Ujimitsu."

The fighting stopped. The ghosts paused in their assault, hateful eyes turned toward Tadaka. He was shouting, his agarwood rod clenched in both hands. "Oh kami, these ghosts defile your shrine!" he shouted. "They disgrace your presence! Will you do nothing? Expel them! Force them out of your sacred home! I beg you!"

As the ghosts leapt, Tadaka broke the rod in two.

The wooden floorboards beneath Tadaka's feet splintered and broke. A shimenawa rope snapped, cracking like a whip. It decapitated six ghosts, which dissolved into fog. Another snapped, banishing three more. A beam fell, the resulting shockwave scattering the fallen wards, each paper finding a ghostly victim and blinking it out of existence with just a touch.

In the pandemonium, the ateru lifted the bone-hilted dagger from the box. As he fed it into a sheath at his hip, less light seemed to pass through him. Then, a whiplike crack of a snapped shimenawa split him in two, breaking him into coils of fading smoke.

As the room finally stilled, Tadaka pulled a small book from the collar of his *haori* jacket. He flung it open, found a page, and tore it out. Flinging the book aside, he held the page aloft, shouted an incomprehensible word, and slammed the page onto the floor in front of him. More floorboards cracked. Something cold ran through Tsukune. Tears bubbled up from her eyes.

Silence. The ghosts were gone. Rainwater trickled from a crack in the ceiling. Wind stirred the singed and tattered wards. Lanterns hung split and jagged like limp jaws, and the scent of burnt oil lingered in the air. Only the well remained pristine and untouched, a grave marker in a quiet battlefield.

Tadaka fell to his knee. Tsukune rushed forward, fearing the worst—that one of the vengeful ghosts had managed to reach him. He staved her off with an outthrust hand. "I'm fine!" he barked, and then more softly, "I need only a moment." His hand came away from the paper he had slammed onto the floor. It was a simple illustrated page, but when Tsukune tried to read it, her vision blurred from unbidden tears.

"It is from the Radiant Sutra," Tadaka explained. "It contains a truth so painful that lost souls cannot bear to be near it. It will keep the ghosts away for now. But it will not last."

A thin red line traced down from Tadaka's lips. He touched the blood with a fingertip, then reached into his mouth and pulled out a broken tooth. It steamed, disintegrating in his palm.

"What have you done?" Tsukune whispered.

He could barely stand. "Our bodies are merely vessels composed of the five elements. To empower the earth kami of this shrine, I offered some earth of my own."

She went numb. "Where did you learn that?" came her hollow voice.

The kami and the Fortunes were not the only spirits that could answer prayers. There were darker forces in the world, forces that granted terrible power. They listened to any who reached for them, shugenja or no. But they accepted only blood. They stained the soul.

Had he learned this trick from his Shadowlands studies?

He seemed to read her thoughts. "I know how it looks. But it is not blood magic."

She looked at him meaningfully. "I can see how one might make that mistake."

He didn't reply.

Tsukune sheathed Ofushikai and gazed around. There were no survivors among the shrine keepers. Kosori hovered over Nobukai against the wall. "He's injured." She bound the daimyō's stump with his sleeve, but the red there was spreading at an alarming rate. "Hold still. Almost done."

"Don't waste your effort," Nobukai managed. "My life is finished."

"We need you," Kosori pleaded. "No one else can string Mikazuki."

"Look at me! I will never string a bow again."

She wrapped another cloth around the wound, almost frenzied. "The Agasha make wondrous prosthetics," she said. "I heard it from a guest once! Cypress wood. Ball-socket wrists with exchangeable hands. The Dragon would surely—"

"Kosori-san."

She stopped.

He gave no expression. "The art of archery is the art of letting go."

She fell away from him, trembling like a brittle leaf.

"I should never have meddled in this," Tsukune whispered.

Nobukai looked at her plainly. Razor cuts littered his face, and his right eye was dark crimson. "Spilled water will not return to the tray. What matters now is stopping him." He sighed. "And I fear you will have to do it alone."

Kosori's eyes popped open. "Maezawa-sama!" she cried. "He can heal you! He is of the Asako family. That's what they do. Maezawa will treat your wounds and—"

"Maezawa is not here," Tadaka observed.

Tsukune rose. He was not among the bodies. Had he even been here during the battle?

From outside, over the sound of the rain, came a loud snap, and then a cascade of crashes.

Tsukune sprinted through the shrine and into the falling sheets of rain. Each frenzied step brought another pang of growing dread. She skidded beneath the torii arch just as a second snap sounded, and the bridge crashed into the gaping ravine.

Maezawa stood on the other side. Even between the layered sheets of rain, a flash of lightning illuminated the serrated dagger he had hidden in his pipe and now held above his grim, weathered face.

"You've killed us!" Tsukune cried. But the thunder stole her words.

The old man shrugged with a remorseful look. Then, he turned away. The last she saw of him was the crest of the Asako on his back.

Tsukune stared at the space where the bridge had stood. Another flash illuminated the valley below. From that gash in the earth, she swore she heard a rush of tangled whispers.

Chapter Seven

"*M*aezawa cut the bridge," said Tsukune.

Kosori's damp eyes widened. Tadaka paled.

Nobukai laughed weakly. The red stain no longer spread, but his eyelids drooped and every breath dragged between his pale lips. "It is too bad you could not convince Tadaka-sama to leave, Tsukune-sama. Otherwise we might have lived beyond tonight."

Tsukune straightened. Nobukai had suggested the waterfall. Asako Maezawa had been waiting for her there. Talking to Tadaka had been his suggestion. "You were working together."

He closed his eyes. "I did not want to involve more outsiders. This is a Kaito family matter."

Her blood boiled. Was it simply the role of the Phoenix Clan Champion to be manipulated by everyone around her? Was this all they thought she was good for?

"Uncle," Kosori asked, "is there another way out?"

Nobukai shook his head. His words came in labored rasps. "This place was built to imprison the ateru. The bridge is the last defense. He has no feet, yet must walk regardless. That is part of his curse."

Wheels turned in Tadaka's head, his prayer beads clicking as he rotated them. "Yes. That's right. Onryō are a kind of ghost. So they cannot pass through salt circles, and they must avoid a lantern's light, and they are stronger at certain hours and weaker during others..."

"You forget," Nobukai interrupted. "Other ghosts are punished by their sins. Onryō exist to punish the living. Such weaknesses do not apply to them." Seeing Tadaka's grim reaction, Nobukai laughed again. "It seems you have tested this water's depth with both feet, Tadaka-sama. I see now why Master Rujo thinks you are not ready."

Tadaka's eyes flashed. "What do you know about it?"

"We are a vassal family with a minor purpose far from civilization. The only reason the council would have sent you here would be as punishment. I wonder how you earned their ire."

So that was why the council sent Tadaka to this place. For challenging his own sensei, they wanted to teach him a lesson.

Amusement twinkled in Nobukai's weakening eyes. "You thought this place was taken by Jigoku, and I a mahō-tsukai. But you merely saw what you wanted to see. It is Tōshigoku that has claimed this place. Adjust your strategy accordingly."

Tōshigoku, the Realm of Slaughter, was a place of perpetual battle. Those who died with thoughts of revenge ended up there, compelled to fight senselessly for all eternity.

Tadaka bent until he was eye to eye with the fallen daimyō. "Crickets are breathing, Lord Nobukai." His gaze softened. "It is unwise to speak of those realms while so close to death, lest one of them take you."

"Speak of them I must! I must tell you what you are up against!" He gasped, eyes popping open. "But now there is no time."

Tears streamed down Kosori's face. "This is my fault."

"No," Nobukai said. "I am to blame. Me and my hubris." He coughed. His voice weakened. "I saw your efforts. The tags, the wards... But you are not strong enough to replace an Elemental Master, nor can you replicate the knowledge our family lost when we joined the Isawa."

Kosori's brow pinched. "But we came from the Isawa..."

"There is much you do not know," he continued, "but I have taught you none of it. I should have included you, told you what I was doing. I thought instead that I could spare you the danger, the pain..." He scoffed. "But I was foolish. Sun Tao once said, 'Try to save your soldiers, they will die. Plunge them into danger, they will live."

Tadaka prayed. "Emma-o, Fortune of Death, judge this soul fairly and lead him to his next reward…"

"Seek our past," Nobukai gasped. "Therein lies our future! Promise me, Kosori!"

Still grasping his hand, she nodded, her tears scattering like the ocean's spray.

He leaned back and whispered:

"Old men would tell me
That death carried a blindfold
And I believed them.
Yet with open eyes, I see
His lantern, like the sun, sets."

Kaito no Isawa Nobukai breathed no longer. Kosori's head sank to her shoulders. She trembled, sniffling, as the rain fell outside.

"Cry, and he will hear you," Tadaka said.

She stopped.

"Cry, and he will remain, trying to comfort you. Bodiless, formless, never moving on to the next world. For him, you must endure."

Kosori stood and wiped her face with her forearm. "You killed him."

Tadaka held very still.

Her words came through clenched teeth. "If you hadn't stormed in here, none of this would have happened."

Tadaka stood to his full height, his shadow expanding against the wall. His eyes narrowed. "My orders come from the council. Choose your words wisely."

Kosori did not back down. She leaned in, fists clenched and shaking.

"Enough!" Tsukune shouted. "It's my fault. Look no further for the one to blame!"

They turned as one.

She was panting. She couldn't stop. Frenzied breaths tumbled from her dry mouth. She was shaking. Why was she shaking? Why did she think she could do this? What had possessed her to draw the sword? Now they were trapped. She'd trapped them. They would die here. Her eyes darted from one body to the next. Their blood was on her hands like a red iron weight coating her palms, dragging her, pushing her through the floor. Falling. Flying. An abyss.

"What's happening to her?" came Kosori's voice, but it was far away. Tsukune sat. She couldn't speak. She couldn't breathe. She was drowning, and the world was darkening, and she was empty, and everything was empty, and everything was broken, and nothing mattered, and—

"Tsukune!"

She jolted. Tadaka's face was inches away. His eyes were calm pools.

"We practiced for this," he said, soothing. "Do you remember? Breathe."

He inhaled. He exhaled. With his next breath, Tsukune followed. Inhaling. Exhaling. Slowly, again. With each breath the floor seemed a little more solid beneath her. She felt in control again. He smiled, relieved. In that moment, it almost felt like the months before. Like nothing had changed. But then his smile wavered, as if in realization, and the moment was gone.

She rose to her feet, accepting his help. Her heart still raced, her chest was tight, and she felt as if she'd been running for hours. But her thoughts were hers again. Kosori's heavy gaze was crushing. She looked as though she'd just watched Tsukune fall into a bottomless pit. In some ways, she had.

Tsukune spoke breathlessly, struggling around her continued panting. "I broke the wards. I passed through the forbidden screen. Whatever wall held the onryō back, I am the one who tore it down."

Do not rest in your own blame.

Tsukune's breath caught. Dim light glinted off Ofushikai's pearls.

"It was bound to happen," Tadaka said. "In any case, you did not thaw the well; I believe that is ultimately what freed them. The rest was inevitable."

We are but petals caught in the spring wind. We cannot say where we will land.

Tsukune regarded Kosori's confused face. "Even so, I acted without thinking. I have wronged you, Kosori. I am sorry."

Kosori looked away. "I…I need a moment."

Tsukune lowered her head as the girl left the room. Cold rain dripped from the ceiling, dabbing her cheek. She hadn't wanted Kosori to see her like that. It had been months since the last time.

But nothing could be done about it now.

"What do we do?" she asked.

Tadaka folded his arms. "Spirits from the Realm of Slaughter are not my expertise, but the key to exorcising any ghost is understanding them. This is what we can safely assume: this shrine was meant to keep this so-called 'ateru' weak." He chewed around the rural word. "What I attributed to Jigoku's corrupting touch was actually the onryō's hatred slowly eroding the wards over time. The dagger, which I had mistaken for an artifact of Jigoku, must instead be one of Tōshigoku."

"What about the other ghosts?" Tsukune asked. "Who are they? Kaito's story told only of one demon. It makes no mention of any others."

"They are also onryō," Tadaka replied. "But lesser than him. It is as if—"

He stopped. The air was suddenly thick. Warm. A faint echo rippled through the shrine. Tsukune's skin broke out in goose pimples at the sound. It was laughter.

An orb blinked into being, a globe of sickly purple flame floating at the center of the room.

Tadaka paled. "Impossible. Could he have worn out the sutra already?"

A dozen more burst into being, casting the room in an unnaturally purple light. Tsukune squinted in the bonfire-like heat. "Behind me!" She grasped Ofushikai's handle, then hesitated. Would drawing it again only make things worse?

"No, behind me." Stepping forward, Tadaka wrapped his prayer beads around his wrist. "I don't care if they are from the Realm of Slaughter! They are still ghosts, susceptible to the sacred substances. Jade will hold them back." He clapped his hands three times. "Kami of earth, become like—"

His voiced trailed. He dropped his posture and thrust his hand into his drawstring pouch for a handful of coins, which he tossed on the floor. He gasped. "They're gone."

"Gone?" Tsukune started. "Who? The kami?"

The flames expanded, taking vaguely humanoid shapes.

Urgently, Tadaka clapped. It was as if he were applauding the floating balls in some bizarre performance. He was trying to attract the kami's attention. She caught his a desperate look. "An offering! Something!"

She yanked the offerings bag from her obi. It wouldn't be enough.

Shadows danced across the wall. She scoured the destroyed room, throwing aside shelves and broken drawers. Empty. Nothing. This was a shrine—how could there be no more offerings?

"Forget it!" Tadaka shouted. He reached into his collar and jerked, snapping a thin strap from around his neck. The amulet in his palm, a green- and white-ribboned carving of a pheasant, shone with glossy light. Jade. Tadaka thrust the bauble into his coin pouch, drew it shut, then smashed a stone offering bowl onto the bag, over and over.

Movement behind her. Tsukune whirled. Kosori stood in the door, her face painted lavender. Tsukune looked back to the flames. "Go, Kosori! We'll hold them as long as we—"

The flames peeled away from the emaciated bodies, their burial clothes flowing in tandem with their wild hair. Their eyes burned behind their death masks.

Kosori darted for the corner as Tsukune grabbed Ofushikai. The ateru materialized, the bone dagger still in his sheath. His shark smile glinted under his long mustache.

Tadaka sprang to his feet. His amulet's remains, a mound of green powder, was cupped in his hand. Jade powder. He thrust it before him. The ateru's eyes narrowed. The ghosts hesitated.

"This is enough jade to tear all of you from the human realm!" he announced. "Take so much as a step, and I will—"

The ateru made a dismissive gesture. A gust scattered the jade powder into a dark corner. Tadaka blinked at his empty palm.

The ghosts laughed. The sound tore at Tsukune's ears and made her blood thick.

Tadaka clenched his fists. "Very well! Come all at once! I won't be humbled! Not by anyone!"

The leader floated forward. He spoke. His speech was thick with an unfamiliar accent, his voice echoing as though through a narrow tunnel. "I am Ateru," he said. "Because you have amused me, I will make you a deal. Give us the girl, and you may leave."

The girl. Kosori.

"You can't have her," Tsukune said, gripping her sword. "I'll take your heads first."

Tadaka pulled a palm-length cylinder of wood from his obi. A *yawara*, his last resort. He made a fist around it. Nothing more needed to be said.

The ateru drew his knife. "Then die."

The spectral wave rushed forward. Tsukune braced for death.

Kosori stepped between them, a strung bow in her hand. She plucked the string. Then, the ghosts were gone.

Tsukune blinked at the moonlit room, not yet lowering her guard. But no attack came. Kosori lowered the bow. "A plucked bowstring can banish evil spirits," she said. "Even so, I wasn't sure it would work."

Tsukune relaxed. "You saved our lives."

Tadaka regarded the girl with wondering eyes. "You strung that bow? Just now?"

Kosori nodded. When Tadaka's expression did not change, she regarded the weapon more closely. Only then did Tsukune notice how old it appeared, the silk tassels adorning its curve, and its glittering bell. Mikazuki.

The realization hit Kosori like a thunderbolt. She tossed the bow like a hot iron. It landed in Tsukune's grip. The string snapped, nearly grazing Tsukune's cheek.

"I…I didn't mean to!" Kosori blurted. "I just strung the first one I could grab!"

A smile spread over Tsukune's face. "Doesn't this mean…?"

Tadaka nodded. "So that is why they wanted you. They hate the Kaito, and you are the Kaito family daimyō."

All color drained from Kosori's face.

Tsukune placed the bow in Kosori's limp hands. The girl just stared ahead, as if in a trance. It was a look, a feeling, Tsukune remembered well.

"We cannot fight them forever," Tadaka said as he gathered his fallen trinkets. "I must realign." They followed him to the main chamber. The rain was slowing, the wind stirring the hanging streamers. He sat in the lotus position, meditating.

Kosori seemed to be in a daze at the shrine's entrance, listening to the rain, hugging the ancestral bow. Her shoulders sagged listlessly, dark bags forming beneath her eyes. She was the future of the Kaito, fragile and flickering like a candle in the mountain's storm.

Tsukune gripped Ofushikai. She closed her eyes. She stood in a circle of peers within the shrine to Shiba as they passed the ancient blade from one to the other beneath the watchful eyes of the Void Master. The sword came to her, a woman with no glories to claim. She had never wanted them. She had anticipated a humble future: a peaceful life and a warrior's death were all she had ever desired. She extended the sword to Shiba Tetsu, Ujimitsu's own apprentice, and his eyes lit upon seeing its exquisite sheath. She knew the blade would choose him. Instead, it unsheathed itself in her hands.

She had wanted to protest, to say it was a mistake. But how could she question the Master of Void? And then she was alone beneath the statue of Shiba, her breath lost and her mind racing. Her rough hands were unfit to hold such a splendid blade. She could never be champion. She could never do this alone.

She remembered the hand on her shoulder. Drawing the blade. Seeing her reflection, and generations of Phoenix Clan Champions, their glowing bodies filtering the moonlight and casting no shadows.

You will never be alone, Tsukune.

Kosori's voice rose in the quiet chamber. It grew in strength, the noise of the rain seeming to match the tempo of her song:

Do not cry, young maple tree
Although the storm strips your leaves.
They paint Sazanami Lake
In such bright colors!

Do not cry, Taiko River
Although the stones divide you.
Someday the endless ocean
Will join you again!

Tsukune opened her eyes. She wasn't going to let this be the end. Not while her heart still beat and she still drew breath.

When Kosori was quiet again, and the rain prevailed, Tadaka rose from his meditation. "The kami have returned." He looked to Kosori, then bowed his head. "My thanks."

Tsukune blinked at her. Kosori's song, had it called the kami back to the shrine?

For her part, Kosori seemed only mildly surprised at Tadaka's praise. Whatever resentment she had felt, she seemed to have set it aside. "What's the plan?" she asked.

"I will attempt to consecrate the shrine. It will no doubt be temporary, but we have few other options." He began taking scrolls from his satchel, unfurling them, and laying them at his feet. "Onryō are beings of extreme emotion. Their desire for slaughter offends the kami, who flee for more harmonious places. To succeed, I must convince the earth kami to remain. This will hold the onryō in place."

"What should we do?"

"String your bow," Tadaka replied. "Otherwise, nothing. I must do this alone."

Tsukune frowned. "Is there truly no way to help? Kosori's wards were powerful: you said this yourself. And surely I can at least search again for offerings?"

"Mere wards will not be of use. As for offerings…"

The steaming tooth. "No. Find another way."

"To consecrate this entire shrine at once, under these circumstances, would otherwise require a pile of offerings! If my technique, my research, can restore the balance here—"

"I forbid it."

He scoffed. "You forbid it? Really?" He crossed his arms. At his full height, the ceiling streamers nearly grazed his forehead. "Can you stop me?"

They both already knew the answer to that question. He would do whatever he wished. In this, and when they were together, he always had to be in control.

"Maybe I was never your yōjimbō," she whispered. "After all, you never let me save you."

His expression softened.

A resounding snap. The shimenawa at the entrance broke, swinging in two pieces. The paper streamers fluttered to the floor.

The room filled with floating orbs, painting the room in flickering iris. Tadaka cursed. Tsukune spun. Kosori lifted the bow. Her panic-lit face said everything. No string.

Tadaka grimly stepped into the center of the room. "Take the scrolls. Close the doors."

Unhesitating, Kosori scooped them up, scrambling to hold them all and her bow.

Tsukune grabbed his arm. "You can't—"

"You'll have to find a way to reconsecrate the shrine," he barked. "You and Kosori. I'll buy you as much time as I can."

The purpose of the yōjimbō was to die in place of their charge. A Shiba served their Isawa for life. She planted herself like a flag at his side.

He shoved her back. "You can't help me!" The pale light painted his desperate eyes.

"It should be me instead!" she shouted. "I'm your yōjimbō, whether you like it or not!"

"It's got nothing to do with that!" Tadaka barked back. "What will become of Ofushikai if you fall here? What will become of the Phoenix?"

Tsukune gritted her teeth. Ghostly forms encircled them.

"Is this a good time to argue?" Kosori asked, one foot halfway into the inner shrine.

Tadaka's shadow was tossed between flickering lights. As the flames increased, it grew darker. "What use am I otherwise?" Tsukune said. "At least let me do what I was trained to do! Someone else, someone more worthy, will become champion."

Tadaka's face broke into an anguished scowl. "Damn you, Tsukune! If you would only look past your own nose, you would see you are destined for this! That the sword chose wisely!"

Her gasp snuffed out her anger. He turned his back, his voice carrying a hesitant sting. "The way your peers look at you. How deeply you care about them. I will never have what you have." His voice wavered. "What you inspire in others is far greater than any feat you could accomplish alone. So imagine what you could do if you were inspired by yourself!"

Now he was saying this. Here. In these circumstances, when she needed to be strong. "*Baka*," she whispered, a wet line trailing down her cheek.

As she followed Kosori away, beneath the crackling flames and steadily growing screams of otherworldly voices, she swore she heard his quiet murmuring. As she closed the shōji doors, she saw Isawa Tadaka as a silhouette wreathed in jade flames. She shut the screen so forcefully, it cracked the frame. Then, silence.

You just killed him, she thought. *You killed him to save your own skin.* She clenched her teeth through a swelling film of tears. *Damn you, Tsukune. You're no better than Maezawa.*

Kosori dropped the scrolls and made for one of the keepers' bodies. There would be a bowstring there. Tsukune watched, swallowing around a lump in her throat. She blinked her tears away. *Kosori is what matters now. You must protect her.*

A flash of violet light. And there was the ateru, floating just before the well. Kosori froze, her eyes flicking to a bowstring just inches away. He followed her gaze and laid a hand on the bone-handled dagger.

"Go on," he said, jaw unhinging, voice echoing. "Try."

She steeled her gaze. "What do you want from me?"

His eyes burned hatefully. "The Kaito have forgotten, have they? That changes nothing. I have lost track of the hundreds of years I've waited for this moment. Nothing will sway me." A wreath of flames surrounded him. The room became a furnace. "If I have to cleave the mountain, I will see Momotsukihime's children utterly eradicated!" He drew his blade. "Starting with you!"

The first lesson of the Shiba yōjimbō was simple, yet overlooked by other schools. To be a good bodyguard, one needed not impressive defenses, nor speed to outpace the attacker, nor even the ability to detect danger. One needed only one thing: to be the greater of two threats. Tsukune screamed and threw herself upon him.

The ghost stepped out of her reach, but she did not relent. She ignored the burning in her joints and pressed forward. She needed only to buy Kosori time to string the bow. Nothing else mattered. She struck, again. Again.

He pinned her arm midstrike and drove the dagger into her shoulder.

The blade was a fire inside her. There was light behind her eyes, and for a moment, the world was an infinite battlefield stretching in all directions beneath a fire-brimmed sky.

Kosori strung the bow. She plucked.

The shockwave yanked the ghost away. The dagger carved a path through Tsukune, an arc of red splashing against the wall. Tsukune's strength left her. She stumbled, her head thudding hard against the roof of the well. She tumbled in. The water swallowed her up.

Dimly, she thought to swim. Her arms did not obey. Through her blurry vision, she saw a wavering portal above and a face that might have been Kosori's. It grew smaller and smaller.

Sinking, she thought. But she was too tired to care. The water was cool and dark. A red, cloudy trail followed her down. She felt that she was a part of it now.

Distantly, Kosori called her name. Then, she heard nothing at all.

Chapter Eight

*T*sukune.

She scrunched her face. The voice was not her father, but it sounded like a father's voice. Concern and strictness and love.

You are sinking.

She didn't care. It was cool here. Quiet. The water soothed her aching limbs, cooled her tired eyes, and dulled all sensation, even the distant ache of her shoulder.

Wake up.

Why? It was still dark. Too early to awaken, too early—

AWAKEN.

Tsukune's eyes popped open. She was suspended in a wide octagonal shaft. Faint light filtered from above and below. Drowning. She was drowning!

She thrashed. Her lungs were bursting. Which way was up? The light dimmed. The paper balloon inside her tore open, and as the urge to breathe won control, she felt a final pang of shame. Hundreds of Phoenix Clan Champions, and she would be the first to lose the ancestral sword. It would fall from her limp fingers to the bottom. For that reason alone, this was a fitting end. Better that she should sink and never be seen again.

Her mouth opened. She inhaled. The water rushed in.

At first she thought she was dreaming. She had breathed in oceans while dreaming before. But then her shoulder throbbed in hot pain. This was real.

From the first breath, she didn't stop inhaling. A steady stream of bubbles blew from her nostrils as she endlessly drank. Her water-filled lungs made her heavy and full, while the dreamlike quiet dark washed away all urgency.

Ofushikai. She would have gasped if she were not perpetually doing so. The iridescent pearls of its grip were glowing. The sword seemed more alive here, the wooden sheath young and newly carved, a gossamer aura refracting the filtered light. She drew the sword partway and watched thin shadows dancing on the gleaming steel, as if it were beneath the ocean shallows.

When the Empire was new, Shiba fell in love with a woman from beneath the sea, a mermaid named Tsumaru. Because she was a princess, their marriage briefly united the undersea kingdom of the Ningyo with the fledgling Shiba family. But as the years passed, she grew weak from her time away from the sea. After the Day of Thunder, when Shiba vanished in the Shadowlands, she dove into the sea below the cliffs of Castle Shiba, becoming a fish by the time she broke the waters.

The story from Tsukune's childhood replayed itself in her grandmother's voice, revealing one final detail. On their wedding day, Tsumaru presented a gift: a sword, forged by her own hands, using metals and techniques from the kingdom beneath the sea. This sword she named Ofushikai, a Ningyo word with an esoteric meaning. Tsumaru had made a sword that was stronger beneath the waves and allowed its wielder to breathe water as if it were air, because she knew she would someday return to the ocean. And when that day came, she wanted her husband to visit her.

A glowing bubble broke Tsukune's reverie. Far below was a dim light. Returning the sword to its sheath, Tsukune swam down, mouth agape like a fish. The water grew warmer, and the light, a sickly purple, grew steadily brighter.

The bottom of the well was a box-shaped room, well lit, although Tsukune could not find the source. The water was like an *onsen*, hot and still. She had the sensation that she was standing in a doorway, both inside and outside. The walls were mortared stone, but now and again, whenever the light flickered, they seemed to vanish, revealing an infinite crow-picked battlefield. Her wound burned whenever it appeared.

She tensed. There was a body, waterlogged and swollen, staring sightlessly at the top of the shaft. It was mostly intact and well preserved. Its clothing was unfamiliar in origin, of fibrous cloth and leather belts. It had a strong jawline and a long mustache. There was fire tattooed on the man's mummified face. His hair was stacked into an elongated bun at the top of his head. A dagger sheath, bone white, was like a beacon against his black tunic. But there was no dagger. In his chest was an arrow, protruding like a planted flag.

So this was the ateru banished by Isawa Kaito. Preserved by the ice for hundreds of years. Not a demon, but a human being.

A gentle current brushed her cheek. She followed it to a small opening, just large enough to squirm through. The source of the well.

She swam slowly and for some time. The tunnel grew dark, only the faint light of Ofushikai's pearls revealing the smooth stone walls polished by the current. At last the floor ramped upward, and reaching, her arm broke the water's surface. She stood.

Ofushikai's light barely revealed an underground cavern. Tsukune had come up in the shallows of a subterranean river. A distant echo suggested waterfalls or cascades. She was in some hidden chamber beneath the shrine. Or so she hoped.

She sputtered. Bending over on mossy ground, she exhaled a steady stream, her lungs emptying, until she was coughing, the noise echoing through the cavern. A cacophony of screeches signaled disturbed bats. She gasped a lungful of musty air. As she did, Ofushikai's light blinked out, leaving her in pitch dark.

She lay on her back, gasping, succumbing to her aches and pains. She was soaked and heavy and without the strength to move. A fire burned inside her arm socket. But her heart still beat. Was she really still alive? Had the Fortunes spared her in this forsaken place?

She laughed, sputtering, the cavern drinking the sound. No one would believe this, not Kosori, not…

Tsukune bolted up. Kosori. Tadaka. They were still in the shrine somewhere, fighting. Dying. She could not stay here.

As she achingly rose, the stalactites and rock formations dimly appeared before her. She thought her eyes had adjusted, but then she saw dancing shadows. There was a winding trail of candles leading deeper into the cave. Not knowing where else to go, she followed it with soggy steps. As she walked, candles spontaneously lit ahead of her, while those behind snuffed out.

They led her to a hollow chamber. A sudden flash assailed her as hundreds of candles lit at once. Shimenawa ropes with lightning-shaped tassels hugged stalagmites or swayed from a stone torii arch. A shrine was carved into the wall, decorated with ropes and dozens of tiny bells. Within the shrine sat a stone urn. Three hallways led deeper into this underground shrine.

She paused. Where did she go from here? Somewhere above, Tadaka was locked in a battle of wills with dozens of ghosts, and Kosori was alone with no one to defend her. Yet her urgency melted here, as if she had stepped into a place where time had no meaning.

The candlelight shifted from yellow to blue. Her hand darted to the sword, but her yōjimbō haragei was calm. There was no danger. As she relaxed, a pinprick of blue light coalesced before the shrine. It rapidly unfolded into a suit of glowing armor. Tsukune paused at the familiar heraldry, recognizing the one who wore it, his kind eyes as iridescent as the sword's pearls.

"Ujimitsu."

She fell to her knees and placed her forehead on the ground. The spirit watched, saying nothing. She searched for words, but nothing seemed right to say. She had no secrets from him; he had been in the sword's reflection that day at Shiba's shrine, he had deflected the ghost's attack meant for her throat. He was never far from the sword, it seemed. Surely he had seen everything she had done.

"You have come to judge me," she uttered. "Very well. I know… that I am unworthy. I ruined the sanctity of the shrine. I freed an angry ghost. Priests are dead because of my actions. There is nothing I can do to atone." She offered the blade. "Please, find one more worthy. It should not be too challenging."

He approached, his hand hovering above the surrendered blade. *It is for the best,* she thought. She would make the four cuts when this was over.

Ignoring the sword, Ujimitsu's spirit laid his hand on her forehead.

Her world vanished.

"I see you both are acclimating. In time, you will unlock Ofushikai's full abilities."

Tsukune stood in the Chamber of the Elemental Masters. There was the circular table with the five seats, the brilliant tapestries of the Elemental Academies hanging from the walls. How had she gotten here?

"Has it spoken to you?"

She turned toward the voice and recognized Isawa Ujina. Only gray had not yet stroked the temples of the Master of Void, nor had wrinkles yet set into his face. He tilted his head, expecting an answer.

She hesitated, then opened her mouth to reply.

"It has," came another voice.

Ujina had not been looking at her. He was looking *through* her.

Behind her, she saw a shorter man in elaborate wing-shouldered robes, topknot bobbing above an unremarkable, youthful face. Ujimitsu. Ofushikai rested in his inexpert hands. He didn't seem to notice her.

These events had already unfolded. She was just a spectral bystander to an immutable past.

"I've seen...visions," the young Ujimitsu confessed. "Dreams. I find them disturbing."

"They come from the sword?"

He looked confused. "Where else?"

Ujina nodded. "The Empire is strongest when the clans stand united, but only the Phoenix can show them the threat. You must prepare the clan for that day. That is your purpose."

Ujimitsu's eyes fell to the sword. Tsukune's eyes narrowed. Was he...trembling?

"Why me?" he asked.

Tsukune gasped.

Ujina regarded him curiously. "The sword chooses as it will, Ujimitsu. You know this."

"I am not a warrior. I am a painter! A woodcarver! I make portraits for newlyweds and toys for children!" Anguish washed over Ujimitsu's features. "It should have been Masumi! She is ten times the warrior I am. She understands the Tao where I can only scratch my head. Make her the champion, not me!" In the young champion's expression, Tsukune saw herself.

The Void Master shook his head. "That is not within my power. If the sword were meant for Masumi, it would have chosen her. The sword chose you."

Ujina smiled at him. "If you seek the answer why, look within."

Tsukune blinked. She was in the cavern once more, kneeling before the spirit of Ujimitsu. She blinked tears from her face. Her mind flooded with questions as her fingers curled around Ofushikai. She understood.

"It's your voice," she said. "All this time. You have been calling out to me. When I lose control, you call me back."

"They were your steps, not mine."

Her eyes widened. This voice came not from her mind. It bounced off the cavern walls and made the candles flicker and brighten. But it was the same.

"We are not born worthy. We *become* worthy. Our suffering is a flower, without meaning unless it blooms." He extended his arms like gossamer wings. "The Soul of Shiba knows its own. Trust it. Trust yourself. Be true to who you are and embrace whatever tests you. You will not always win. Repentance does not come first. But you should always try. Like unwrought metal, fearlessly embrace the flames and be changed."

Tsukune's heartbeat thundered through the cavern. Where once had been doubt, now a glowing light prevailed.

"Live. Die. Be reborn." Ujimistu smiled. "That is the way of the Phoenix."

Tsukune rose. She returned Ofushikai to her obi and met Ujimitsu's eyes. "I'll do my best."

The spirit vanished. The candles went out. Tsukune stood in the darkness of the hidden shrine. Soundless. Empty.

But she was not alone. Never alone.

Chapter Nine

The steps rose to Tsukune's feet as she ran, her heart pounding in her ears. Her first guess had been lucky; just a glimpse of spiral stairs leading up was enough to break her into a run. The twist was so narrow she had to take Ofushikai from her obi, lest it drag against the wall. Her body protested with each step, her tight muscles burning. Her shoulder wound had gone numb, the soreness just a hollow echo of before. These thoughts fell to the basement of her mind. They were unimportant, mere pond ripples compared to the sound of rain growing louder as she climbed. In her mind's eye, she saw Tadaka's silhouette as jade flames leapt at his attackers. She saw Kosori alone with the ateru. She pumped her legs harder and prayed to the Fortunes that this stairway would lead back to the shrine. That Tadaka and Kosori, like her, were somehow still alive.

Halfway up, a sound touched her ears. She stopped, straining to hear over the noise of her breathless panting. It was singing. Faint, distant, but clear. A rustic tune. Kosori's voice.

And she was running again, faster than her breath could carry.

The top opened to a square room lit by a masoned window. Sound ravaged the chamber, echoing rain and thunder, though Kosori's voice was still clear. Tsukune sprinted to the far wall, a sliding door with the crest of the Kaito family. She yanked it, but it held shut. Icy daggers shot through her shoulder. She bit back the pain and the sudden rush of warmth against her side, trying again. Something was jammed in the sliding track, pinning it shut. She stepped back. Whispering an apology to whatever spirits watched, she ran and with all her remaining strength threw herself upon the wooden surface.

The door collapsed with a resounding crash. At once came the familiar musty smell of cobwebs and dust, and moonlight flooded in. Tsukune was back in the shrine. She praised the Fortunes.

As she stood, she felt a sudden swoosh by her cheek. An arrow stuck into the doorframe, splintering inches from her face. A second bit her arm and became embedded in the tight fibers of her kimono silk. "Stop!" she shouted hoarsely. "It's me!"

Kosori had just nocked a third arrow and drawn Mikazuki to full extension, the bow curving like the crescent spring moon. She was in the inner shrine. The door Tsukune had broken was the wall panel that backed Mikazuki's bow stand.

Recognition dawned across Kosori's features. "Tsukune?" She lowered the bow. Her face brightened. "Tsukune!"

She was across the room in seconds, arms around Tsukune in a warm embrace. Then Kosori remembered herself and drew back, red-faced. "I...I thought the worst." Her eyes twinkled. "You're alive. You're really alive!"

Tsukune smirked without energy. "So I am told."

"What happened? Where did you come from?"

She gestured limply at the hidden passage.

Kosori spared it only a brief glance before flicking her eyes at Tsukune's shoulder and a stain shades darker than her red silks. "You're bleeding!" she exclaimed.

"Oh?"

Kosori sat her by the well, setting the bow aside. Tsukune placed Ofushikai beside it. A glance at the well revealed her reflection. Waterlogged, with her ponytail undone, her disheveled kimono splotchy and stained, purple rings beneath her eyes, and the arrow protruding from her sleeve, she looked as though she'd crawled out of a watery grave. And, she supposed, she had.

She looked beyond at the complete disarray of the room. Arrows were stuck into rafters and walls. Broken furniture and wards were scattered everywhere. "What happened?"

"They tried to ambush me. They failed."

Tsukune nodded. "Where did you find arrows?"

"Under the floorboards." Kosori gestured. "Lots of stuff down there. Mostly arrows, but some incense and spices too. Some gold plates," she added offhandedly.

"Gold plates? Too bad it wasn't something useful."

Kosori gestured to her shoulder. "Let me see."

"In the shrine? What if my blood touches the floor?"

Kosori made a wry face. "I think we're beyond that now."

Tsukune pulled her arm in through her sleeve and out of her collar. Red painted her shoulder and arm around a gaping wound and purple flesh. "Think it might scar?" she joked.

Kosori winced. "I think it may fall off. How have you not bled out?"

"I think he cauterized it," Tsukune replied. "The blade felt hot."

"Well, it's still bleeding. Although it looks clean." Kosori nodded. "I have just the thing."

As Kosori stepped away, Tsukune closed her eyes and felt the burn beneath her eyelids. Her arms were made of lead; her legs were sand-filled sacks. It had to be close to sunrise by now. Laying her head against the well, she looked at the closed screen separating this room from the main chamber. There was no noise from behind those doors. Nothing at all.

Returning, Kosori followed Tsukune's gaze. "I'm sure he's alright." She offered a stoic expression. Hopeful. "He is the scion of an Elemental Master."

Tsukune nodded. "I'm sure," she replied, ignoring the part of herself that felt this was a lie.

"All right, let's bandage this." Kosori held up a wad that looked like a charcoal-colored ball of cotton.

Tsukune grabbed her wrist. "What is *that*?"

"Cobwebs."

Tsukune gave her an incredulous look.

"It works. See?" Kosori extended her forearm. A vertical gash ran down her arm from palm to elbow. Something thick and clumpy lay against the wound, reddish brown and stuck to the skin. It moved organically with her flesh, like a scab.

Kosori smiled. "I told you spiders in a shrine were good luck!"

When Tsukune could stand, they each took a candle and she led Kosori through the passage in the wall. They descended the spiral stairs, Kosori breathless and wondering. "You did not know this was here?" Tsukune asked.

"If I had, I'd have led us down here. With all the wards and shimenawa, surely the onryō cannot follow."

When they came to the cavern shrine, Kosori's knees struck the ground. "That's Kaito's urn!" She lowered her head. "I never knew where we kept it…"

After her prostrations, they explored the subterranean halls. One led to an armory containing dozens of arrows, some with jade tips and blessings tied to the shafts. Another led to a mushroom garden, a shimenawa encircling a dead log at the center.

The third was where they found the library. Bookshelves divided the room, with more set into the walls. Scroll cases stacked into pyramids filled many shelves. Others contained boxes with books inside. The herby smell of parchment permeated the room.

Kosori set Mikazuki against a wall and darted inside. "There must be thousands!" she proclaimed, her hands grazing the stacks. She peered into a wooden case left slightly ajar. "They're journals!" She lifted one, a coverless hemp-bound book with rustic lettering. "This is the personal journal of Isawa Tsuruko, Kaito's daughter! I didn't know this existed!"

"And these are star maps," Tsukune remarked, gesturing to a line of cylindrical cases that were labeled as such. "It seems the Kaito kept extensive records." On the same shelf sat cases marked with dates, some hundreds of years old. "These must be the histories of the Kaito." She paused. At the end of the shelf was a wooden mask. Tsukune took it. The old wood left dust on her fingertips. Looking into its featureless face, her mind leapt to another place, a village whose name she'd promised to forget. She'd last seen such a mask among the Yobanjin.

At the library's center sat a desk. Numerous documents were scattered across its surface: a floor plan of the shrine, numerous journals, some scrolls. They had been placed here recently. At the head sat an *emakimono*, a scroll combining pictures and text, intended to be unrolled and read horizontally. Kosori revealed the first section, an elaborate depiction of a woman in shrine maiden garments battling a demon. Isawa Kaito. Hands trembling, Kosori read the words aloud.

"If you are reading this, it is surely because you are the daimyō of our family. I leave this document for all future leaders of the Kaito so that they may know our true history." Kosori paused, brow pinching. "When the shrine is complete, I will hide this in the under-sanctum, the secret place my mother so often visited. Her deeds are recounted throughout these provinces, even spoken before the Emperor himself. That story is an incomplete truth. With my heart and mind aligned, I write below the true story of our family's founding…"

Kosori's voice lowered until there was no sound at all. She advanced through the scroll, eyes darting from writing to pictures and back. Her lips trembled, mouthing words. Then, she stopped.

"That's…that's not possible."

Tsukune took the scroll from Kosori's limp hands. It unfurled, scrollbar clattering to the floor. "My mother was born Kaito no Momot-sukihime," Tsukune read, "Princess of the Hyōketsu tribe of…"

The word seized her breath. "Yobanjin."

Kosori stared at Mikazuki. "That's…that's not…"

Tsukune continued. "Among the Hyōketsu, a princess and priestess are one and the same. Although my mother never possessed the gift of shugenja, she was a medium of spirits and the spiritual representative of her tribe. With this came an awesome responsibility to preserve sacred places. She always held this duty in great reverence.

"In her time, famine and misfortune led the Hyōketsu to stage raids against Isawa provinces, raids that grew bolder with every victory. Brief skirmishes to feed the tribe became extended campaigns to steal the wealth of Rokugani. And then came the visitor from their own Imperial Court, who paid the Hyōketsu to run daring attacks throughout Isawa lands…"

Tsukune clenched her jaw. Those words assured that this document could never leave this place. The accusation, levied against an Imperial official, would shame the Emperor.

"'My mother never approved of these raids. She was the lone dissenter among the tribe's leaders, including her betrothed. My mother watched with growing disgust as fields were burned, innocents killed, shrines defiled, and their sacred archery traditions, meant to honor the spirits, were instead converted for violence. She watched war change her people, quietly hating what they had become.

"But the Fortunes are always watching. One day they found the defenders ready; an army of Shiba, supported by Isawa blessings, backed them into a corner.

"This is why, to save her people, my mother betrayed them. In secret, she approached the Isawa with an offer: she would give the raiding tribe to them in exchange for a place among the Phoenix. For this, she and those who followed her became vassals of the Isawa. They were granted land in the mountains of Garanto Province." Tsukune looked up from the scroll. "Assimilation would have meant the death of her people's culture. She willingly chose that rather than let the violence continue."

Kosori's tremulous voice rose from the corner. "All my life, I was told we were Isawa. That our lower station did not matter, because our bloodline was prestigious, our duty sacred, our ways derived from the tribe of Isawa himself!" Tears ran freely down her face. "They were lies. We are conquered Yobanjin, founded by a betrayal! We were never Isawa. We are not even Phoenix."

Silence hung thick between them.

"Is that what you think?" Tsukune finally said. "What does this change? You are still children of the Phoenix, no matter your origins."

"Adopted children," she replied bitterly.

"Does that matter? Mikazuki does not seem to care. Why should I?" She leaned in, meeting the girl's wet stare. "I told you that I have seen Yobanjin, Kosori-san. When I did, I couldn't help but think they were not so different from us."

"The Elemental Masters might not see it that way."

The Asako heal, the Shiba protect, and the Isawa…know.

"I'd imagine they already know," Tsukune replied. Perhaps they already knew everything. The onryō. The eroding wards. They had sent Tadaka to punish him…but could she say they had not also anticipated this and sent him to stop it?

For that matter, had the Master of Void sent her, too? With the histories unfurled before her, it was impossible to tell what was due to guiding hands and what was merely fate.

Tsukune continued reading. "My mother's decision bypassed the council and was seen as treasonous. The Hyōketsu, like all Yobanjin, valued freedom over all else. Many would not bend their knee to their ancestral enemies. Among those who refused to join was my mother's betrothed: Ateru, the Demon of Wyvern Pass."

"Ateru," she repeated. The realization was like the final placement of a Go piece. "It's his name."

Tsukune knew the rest even before the scroll told her. Ateru could not forgive the betrayal. In his eyes, she'd laid their very identity at the altar of the Isawa, selling out her own people. She was a defector. The insult could never stand. And so, long after Kaito had taken an Isawa husband and established her line, he led the remaining Hyōketsu against her. Her death would wipe the disgrace from his people.

The body in the well. The arrow in its chest. The dagger...

"She didn't kill a demon," she murmured. "She killed her betrothed. Ateru. And with time, the true history forgotten, his name came to mean 'demon' in your dialect." Her chest tightened. "No wonder Ateru hates the Kaito. Betrayed, he died by her hand, never achieving his justice. He died lusting for revenge and was forgotten. His hatred must have..."

The flickering walls within the well. The infinite battlefield.

"...flung him into Tōshigoku. Kaito gave her life to trap him. He's been frozen down there all these centuries, with all his followers, the entire Hyōketsu, as..."

Their screaming masked faces. Their reaching hands.

"Onryō." She paled. "He must have clawed his way back. And Tōshigoku is still waiting for him. That's what he wants. The destruction of the Kaito. Nothing less will do."

Kosori's eyes wavered. She was trembling. Tsukune watched the anguish crawl over her face, tanned and soft-featured, a far cry from those common to the Isawa. Grabbing the bow, she ran from the room, knocking the wooden case of journals off its perch. Books spilled across the floor.

Tsukune started to follow, but stopped. Tsuruko's journal had fallen open on a specific page, one visited so often the spine bent there naturally. Her eyes automatically read the practiced strokes in the Phoenix Clan cipher:

Again I am awakened by Ateru's screams.

I have lost track of how many nights his cries and demands have kept me from sleep. When I do not reply, he lists the ways Mother wronged him. From the well, I hear him even now.

The Elemental Masters say there is little they can do. They could defeat him, but they are unwilling to deploy their power in this way; it would cause more harm than good, disrupting the harmony of the spirit realms. Even a pebble can cause waves. Invoking the earth and fire kami for battle in one place could result in a volcanic eruption elsewhere. No matter how people try to convince themselves that their actions have no repercussions, to turn their heads and deny the consequences, in this world, all things are connected.

Master Gensa is creating shimenawa that will constrain Ateru's reach, and Father's wards will quiet his voice. Gensa-sama warns that this is not a permanent solution. "A gardener who ignores their weeds dooms the garden," he said. Knowing this, I wonder: if Ateru is silenced, will I sleep any better?

– Kaito no Isawa Tsuruko, Month of the Ox, Isawa Calendar year 522

Tsukune found Kosori in the inner sanctum. She was struggling to remove Mikazuki's string, but the bow refused to bend, even when Kosori pressed its arm against the floor.

Kosori noticed Tsukune and paused. "I can use another bow. I don't need to use this one."

Tsukune just watched.

"It will be daylight soon," Kosori continued. "The onryō will vanish in the sun, like a bad dream." She looked at the bow. "I'll unstring it and put it back. Uwazuru will take it. He's a better choice anyways."

"Kosori..." Tsukune spoke.

"You'll tell the Masters about the haunting! They'll fix the wards! Everything will go back to how it was! As if nothing—"

"It doesn't work like that. A launched arrow cannot be withdrawn."

Kosori grimaced. Her eye twitched, oh so slightly. Then her expression broke, twin streams falling from her eyes. She collapsed. On her knees, she hid her face in her hand, shaking from emotion she could not contain. "I can't do this," she whispered. "I can't. Not knowing it was a lie. Not knowing we wronged them. I can't. I'm just not..."

Tsukune's heart twisted. "You have to, Kosori. There's no one else."

Kosori scoffed. "I was the worst in my class. I couldn't fire a bow without striking my cheek. I tried to learn, but nothing stayed in. All I've ever wanted to do is sing. I never wanted to be a shrine maiden! I had dreams!"

It was a shameful admission. Kosori looked away. "The only reason I even passed my shufuku was as a favor to my uncle. I've always burdened him. I shamed him even the moment I was born. Is there anything worse?"

Tsukune tried to smile. "But you've improved so much since then."

"How can I lead when they don't respect me? Uwazuru would be better. It should be him."

Tsukune shook her head. "The bow chose you. It—"

She stopped. The Void Master had said to look within. But he'd been wrong. It was here, in this place, that she finally understood.

"I'm not strong like you, Tsukune-sama." Tearful, Kosori looked into her eyes. "If only I had your courage."

Tsukune froze. The world fell away. *That is how she sees me?*

Like Tsukune had seen Ujimitsu. Strong. Certain. No room in his heart for doubt. The Master of Void had said he was a proactive champion. In every story she'd heard, he never hesitated.

And yet, he'd had his doubts. She knew that now. When the sword chose him, he'd been afraid. But had it made him any less strong? New air filled Tsukune's lungs. No. Moments of weakness did not lessen his legend. Just as Kosori was still strong now, in spite of her doubts. Just as—

She grabbed Kosori's shoulders. Their gazes locked. "Kosori! I am *terrified*!"

Kosori stared, wet eyes unblinking. The words tumbled freely, emptying her, growing lighter each syllable. "I don't know what I am doing. I wasn't ready for this. I wasn't even raised in the Shiba dōjō: I was traded to the Lion, trained as an Akodo until…" Her voice cracked. "…until I had to replace my brother."

"Tsukune…" Kosori murmured.

"I didn't excel. I would never have been anything more than a simple yōjimbō. And I was fine with that! I was happy in Tadaka's shadow! I wanted nothing more!" The emotion faded from Tsukune's face. "But none of that matters. Ofushikai chose *me*."

"And it is shameful to allow that moment to pass with inaction. What is a life but a mere handful of moments? We get so few of them. If I succumb, if I let my doubt drag me down, I will take the fate of my people with me. I cannot, I *will* not let that happen. I must…"

Kosori was smiling. Faintly, but just so. The words, her words, were echoed by voices only she could hear. Ofushikai was glowing.

Tsukune rose. Her voice filled the chamber, bolstered by the voices of countless others who had spoken the same. Hundreds of years shared this moment.

"We are but droplets in the river. We cannot say where the current will take us, for our paths are cast the moment we are born. But sometimes, when we are dashed upon the rocks, we might, for a moment, capture the sun."

A ring of glowing spirits surrounded them. They appeared as they had in life, young and old, expert and untested, ancient and modern. All unified by the same duty. All wearing the same knowing expression. All champions of the Phoenix Clan. Directly across, Ujimitsu nodded. Tsukune matched his smile.

"That is what it means to be a Phoenix."

The spirits were gone. Tsukune's hand grasped Ofushikai's hilt. It fit perfectly.

Kosori picked up her bow and the nearby bundle of arrows. Dark rings still glittered wet beneath her eyes. But there was fire behind them now. "I'll try to be worthy." She rubbed her face with her sleeve. "Sorry I cried."

"That's fine." Tsukune smirked. "You can cry in the dōjō if you laugh on the battlefield."

From the crack between the closed shōji doors came a thin unnatural light.

They saw it simultaneously: a glowing strip increasing in intensity. Tsukune could picture them: dozens of flaming orbs blinking into existence. Ateru was among them. The heat of his hatred seared even this far. She and Kosori exchanged one final look before they turned, resolutely, to the doors. Kosori readied a blessed arrow. Ofushikai sang a brilliant note as Tsukune freed it from the sheath.

The doors burst open.

Chapter Ten

The onryō were a glowing swarm of death. The stage was like a beach, and they were a sea rising to claim it. Tsukune cleaved through four just as they stepped through the doorway. Two more leapt at her exposed back. She made no attempt to duck from harm. Kosori's arrow blinked them away before they could touch her.

Then Tsukune planted herself in the doorframe, where no more than three could come at once. They rushed her in a relentless wave of burning eyes and masked faces. She struck, again and again, while Kosori picked off the ones that gave her trouble. She didn't flinch, not even when an arrow whizzed past her ear. Kosori's heart was beating in Tsukune's chest.

And then she spotted him. Rising above the ethereal throng, Ateru drew his dagger. The ghosts stopped. They appeared as they had in death, rays of light marking their mortal wounds.

Kosori called out. A shaft of purple light emanated from the well. Then came hands and ethereal bodies. The very ghosts they had just defeated.

"What now?" Kosori called out.

Tsukune grimaced. "Uh…"

Then she knew. And because Kosori knew her heart, so did she.

Kosori rushed forward and plucked her empty bowstring. The shockwave tore through the angry dead. The two women wedged through the path she cleared, Tsukune shearing away the last few onryō on the stage. Each slammed a shōji door, Kosori slapping a paper ward upon the screens. The ward stuck, but as the violet light on the other side grew brighter, the ward aged before their eyes.

They surveyed the room. Two dozen coal-fire eyes glared at them, Ateru in the back making twenty-six. Their hatred radiated from them, their ghostly farming implements and barbarian weapons gleaming in their hands. But they didn't charge the stage. It was silent as death, not even the storm outside making a sound.

Lying against the stage was Tadaka. Pale, his hat torn, his face bloody, he drew ragged breaths and didn't move. A fallen section of shimenawa rope, hastily encircled, separated him from the onryō. Tsukune ran instantly to his side, Kosori's arrow banishing the ghost that tried to intercept. Seeing him was like witnessing a sunrise after a prophecy of eternal night.

Tadaka's bruised eye looked up at her. "You look like you stepped out of your own grave."

"Find a mirror," she replied with a relieved smile.

"I couldn't stop them," he whispered. "They just reappear. Too many…"

"Save your energy." Her eyes darted for options.

Another arrow banished an opportunistic attacker. Tsukune leveled her gaze at Ateru. He grinned back with a shark's mouth.

"He's the demon," she remarked. "It is his body in the well. I've seen it."

"Is that so?"

Kosori let another arrow go, this one aimed at Ateru, but he batted it from the sky with a wind gust. His grin widened, splitting his face in two.

"What happens if I banish him?" Tsukune asked Tadaka.

The shugenja stirred. "All the others will vanish. But he'll just reappear."

"What if we last until sunrise?"

"The next evening it will happen all over again. We need a permanent solution."

Ateru's hateful eyes projected a challenge, his dagger flashing otherworldly light.

"It would buy more time." She rose. "I'll do what I can."

The doors to the inner shrine burst open as the ward finally failed. Kosori turned to the sudden rush of ghosts, slapping a paper streamer against the forehead of the first attacker. It popped like a bubble. "Go on!" she said. "I can deal with them."

The ghostly wave parted to let Tsukune through. She led with her sword. Amusement danced with hatred on Ateru's tattooed face as they circled one another. "You should have taken my offer."

Tsukune readied Ofushikai. "That remains to be seen."

They were enclosed in a ring of twisted faces. He took a bold step forward, testing her. She struck back. They both spun, avoiding each other.

"I know what you are, Ateru," she said. "I know why you're doing this."

"And yet you dare to defend them!" Ateru's dagger nicked Tsukune's face. "The children of traitors! What if it had been *your* people they betrayed?"

She jerked back, counter-striking. He danced around her attack and struck again. She barely deflected. He was faster than any human opponent. Her counters seemed to drag, her shoulder burning with every movement. He did not fear Ofushikai. What could she do to him?

His face brightened, looking into her eyes. "Now you're getting it. You can't win. All you know how to do is destroy. What good will that do against me, when I cannot be destroyed?"

"The weaker you are, the louder you bark."

His lips peeled back from shark's teeth. "I'll show you how weak I am."

A loud bang, like a prolonged crack of thunder, shook Tsukune's bones. The ceiling tore itself a jagged maw. Her eyes shut against the sudden curtain of rain.

Her belly wheel spun. She tumbled forward, his dagger edge raking against her ear. The rain droplets sizzled against Ateru's ethereal body.

She deflected a dagger strike intended for her throat, exposing her shoulder. Ateru grabbed it and dug his fingers into the wound.

Tsukune's world bleached as ice and lightning shot through her. She collapsed, numb.

"You're done!" Ateru cried and drove the dagger down.

He yanked it back, away from Kosori's sudden arrow. A second grazed him, sizzling like enflamed paper. From the stage, devoid of enemies, Kosori pointed her final arrow at Ateru. Prayers tumbled from her lips. The arrow was glowing.

The body in the well. The arrow. Tsukune pointed to a spot on his chest. "Kosori! There!"

She let it fly. It struck into Ateru like a planted flag.

A spout of hot flame burst from where it landed. He did not vanish like before. Instead, he screamed. In that moment, Tsukune felt that she stood on the plain of endless battle.

Steam rose from the planted arrow. Ateru's face was like a split lantern. The bones in his back made peaks under his flesh. His body shook with tremors, as if struggling to maintain its form.

"Bitch!" he shrieked. "I will cut you to pieces and send them to Hell!" He pointed the dagger. "There! That is a daughter of the traitor Kaito! She is the one holding us prisoner! The key is in her guts!"

The onryō scrambled for the stage. Kosori pulled Mikazuki into a perfect crescent moon. But this would not save her: the first wave would be banished; the second would tear her apart. Tsukune pushed herself up. A crimson river flowed down her arm. She forced a foot beneath her. *Get up! Flank them! Force them to face you! Now! NOW!*

But she had no time.

The room shook with Ateru's laughter. "Prepare to meet your ancestors!"

"My ancestors," Kosori whispered, eyes lit from within, as if in epiphany.

She sang.

Night always falls first
Inside the valley
The sun so eager
It is always diving down

A ghost froze still. It towered above her in its death shroud, mere inches away, its black hair unfurling, the gash across its chest bleeding spectral light. But no hatred shone behind its mask. Its eyes were confused, regarding Kosori with open wonder.

She spoke to it. "You remember that song, don't you? My grandmother used to sing it for me. She said her grandmother sang it for her."

Another leapt at her, screaming.

We two are like moths
Chasing the round moon
If the sun won't watch
Then we cannot trust ourselves

It slowed to an uncertain trot, its guard lowering. Two more lowered their arms.

"This is a song from our people," Kosori said. "It is a Hyōketsu song. Remember it? Remember who you once were?"

Kosori's song touched all corners of the shrine. The orchid light softened, cooling to a faint blue. Spectral weapons clattered to the floor. Some of the onryō even sat at her feet, like children.

"Your ways were not lost," Kosori said. "Kaito no Momotsuki-hime kept them alive, folding them into the traditions of the shrine keepers and weaving them into folklore. She recorded your names in the family histories. You were not forgotten." She smiled at them. "We are kin. Our people are one. Remember."

The ghosts blinked with recognition. They made to remove their masks.

"Lies," Ateru growled.

Kosori flew into the wall and was pinned by an onryō's hand. It held her by her skull, its hand covering half of her face. Her limbs swung like a doll's. Mikazuki clattered to the floor.

No! Tsukune gritted against the pain, trying to rise. Her legs were wooden boards.

"They killed you," Ateru goaded the vengeful spirit. "They imprisoned you! If it is not true, why can't you leave?"

Kosori sang.

Night always falls first
Inside the valley
The sun so eager
It is always diving down

The ghost let go. Kosori slumped to the floor, shaking. There were spectral burns where the ghost had touched her, luminescent flecks mingling with her birthmark. The ghosts lowered their guard. One clutched its shaking head.

"Kill her," Ateru said.

They climbed on top of her, shrieking, their thumbs pushed into her throat. Moonlight tears fell from their burning eyes.

Kosori croaked weakly. Tsukune could not hear the words.

"Enough!" Ateru leapt on the stage. "She speaks with two tongues! Crush her throat!"

Even as they choked her, she still mouthed the words. Every beat of Tsukune's heart surged urgency into her burning limbs. She pushed through a web of pain. Her eyes met Kosori's.

Instead of desperation, she saw knowing peace, a glimmer of hope.

They cannot be killed. Only appeased.

Of course.

Tsukune held her sword high. "Children of the Hyōketsu! Hear me!"

Spectral heads spun, dozens of coal-fire eyes lighting her at once.

"I am Shiba Tsukune, wielder of Ofushikai, Champion of the Phoenix Clan! I am empowered to speak for the Elemental Masters; my word is law." She gestured to the spectral crowd. "You have been led astray, told that the Kaito have imprisoned you here. But it is your own anguish that ensnares you! The Kaito are your kin, and your ways live on with them."

The ghosts hesitated. Their eyes cleared.

Tsukune sheathed Ofushikai with a resounding snap. "And that makes you Phoenix!"

Tadaka's expression broke into open horror. She pushed this aside. They were onryō. They were Yobanjin. But they were also the Kaito's ancestors. The first ray of sunlight broke through the splintered ceiling, and as it graced the throng, the gossamer Phoenix crest appeared on their spectral clothing. Their masks fell away. They looked no different from Rokugani.

"I hereby acknowledge you as honored ancestors of the Kaito family, to be venerated and worshipped throughout these lands! Please take your rightful place and be remembered forever!"

The onryō vanished, no trace remaining behind.

Amaterasu's golden light touched the shrine in a gilded ray, painting the room in brilliant orange. Tadaka shook his head in disbelief. "How did you know that would work?"

"Kosori is the Kaito daimyō," Tsukune replied. "If she embraced her past, how could I not do the same?"

Coughing, Kosori stood. She smiled at Tsukune from her place on the stage.

Ateru rose behind her.

A cold rush. Tsukune started to yell, to sprint forward, but time fossilized around her. Kosori was smiling through her spectral burns, her eyes serene.

Then a red geyser burst from her neck. She struck the floor like a wet doll.

Heavy hands squeezed Tsukune's lungs. But she didn't hear her own scream. Ateru's knife glistened in the morning light.

"You think this is over?" he hissed. "There is no end to those the Phoenix have wronged!" He spun toward the inner sanctum. "I can always find more!" He bolted, a blur of mauve light, leaping in an arc and splashing into the well.

Tsukune stared at the pool forming around Kosori's unmoving body. It wasn't real. That hadn't just happened. Kosori was supposed to be the Kaito daimyō. She was chosen!

For you, it is "Tsukune-san." We're friends, aren't we?

There was no pain. Her wounds didn't matter. She opened her hand. Ofushikai leapt from the sheath of its own accord. Grasping the hilt, she marched into the inner sanctum. Beneath the waters of the well radiated a stormy violet light. She stepped onto the edge.

"Tsukune!" Tadaka shouted.

He was reaching for her, grasping, eyes flooded and overflowing. She'd never seen him like that before. He'd never really needed her. Had his posturing, his distant manner, been only a façade? Had he taken her for granted? Did he need her after all?

It's too late, she thought. *I'm finishing this.*

She leapt in. Tadaka's voice, calling her name, fell away. The dark waters were cold. Tsukune embraced them.

Chapter Eleven

The well was a black ocean trench.

Ofushikai's pearls were an anglerfish's lure in the inky deep. Water filled Tsukune's lungs. She sank. Reaching out, her hand touched stone, the smooth texture of bricks followed by an unending sheet of cold metamorphic rock. But to her eyes, there was no wall. Only a churning mass of midnight clouds sculpted by sickly flashes, distant fluttering banners above the flashing tips of spears far below her.

Tōshigoku. The word came unbidden. The Realm of Slaughter churned just beyond her palm, as though she were separated by a pane of crystal ice.

"All she had to do was obey."

The voice came from everywhere. Ateru's. Tsukune spun and drew Ofushikai. The void consumed the blade's light.

"She was a mere priestess. What say did she have in matters of war?"

The water rippled. Her wheel was spinning.

"This happened because she stepped out of her place. She is to blame. When she killed me, she didn't even look at my face! She used a bow! A coward's weapon!"

The temperature rose. Hot water bubbled in her lungs. She tried to speak, but without air she had no voice, only bubbles trailing from her nostrils.

"I am an instrument of consequence. I will wipe out the Kaito and destroy all record of their existence. For what she did, for how I suffered, they will be forgotten as I was forgotten."

Her chest swelled. Her voice came like a bubble's pop. "She already paid her price."

The voice fell silent.

"She wanted to stop the senseless killing, your people and mine. She wanted to stop the desecration of sacred places. She knew that if she did nothing, the Hyōketsu would be wiped out. You are blaming her for your own mistakes." Her hands tightened around Ofushikai's hilt. "You are only angry because she wanted equal respect, and you thought that meant taking something from you. You are the one who would not listen. You led the Hyōketsu to their deaths. You don't want justice. You only want revenge."

"Little girl," the voice growled, "there is no difference."

A white flash. Her blood arced in the water. Her jaw cracked against the invisible wall.

Another. A sharp pain in her ribs. She lashed about, but found no opponent. Claws raked her thigh. The silk split and released a stream of red.

A knife hand from above. Her vision flickered. The abyss pulled her.

Ofushikai's reflection. In it, Ateru lunged.

She brought her blade in time to catch his dagger. He pushed, driving her into the wall, pinning her flat. His shark maw opened and she saw screaming faces in his throat. The water boiled around his spectral flesh.

"I have waited long enough! I will have my vengeance! They thought they could bury me down here and forget. But I will not be silenced. My hate lives!" His eyes burned. "They may have forgotten the truth, but they remembered the demon!"

The water bubbled around her blade. Heat seared her cheek, boiling her flesh. Behind the violet cast of his spectral face was a screaming skull.

"And if I must burn every province, so be it! Even if it is raining spears and Jigoku itself has opened, I will wipe her line from

Ningen-dō! *I will not be ignored!*"

He vanished. Tsukune sank, dragging, down to the bottom.

His voice was a whisper now. "Our sins are but shadows we drag along. Kaito's is inescapable. How long is the shadow of the Phoenix, I wonder?"

The floor pressed against her feet. She fell to a knee. Her vision blurred and her strength ebbed from her wounds. Shaking, fragile, she raised her head.

A battle unfolded around her like an animated mural. There were ancient warriors in broken armor, naked skeletons with spears, and dagger-wielding aristocrats still dressed in splendid silks. She saw tattered banners and clan crests: some she recognized, others she didn't. The beings killed each other, again and again, their white eyes wild, their faces without expression. Spectral blood, liquid of glowworm light, ran like a river. There were no sides. There was no reason. They were snakes eating their own tails. Above she saw turning oxcart wheels with screaming faces at their axles, each one set ablaze. Beyond the churning horde, something massive walked among them, snatching up bodies and biting off heads. It almost looked like a giant skeleton, but she could not be sure. All unfolded in complete silence.

Ateru stood between her and unfurled chaos. His back to her, he reached toward the phantom battlefield with his bone-hilted dagger.

"How many do you think will come when I call them? How many here have the Phoenix wronged? Daimyō? Families? Perhaps an entire clan." The dagger glowed. In the flicker of the light, the battlefield seemed less spectral, more real. Closer.

"Hero. Villain. What does it matter? All I care is that they are on my side. I will embrace anyone who hates the Phoenix." He glanced at her. "Look at you. You can't even stand." Back to the battlefield. "You are defeated for the same reason she was. You tried to defend people who were not your own." He held the dagger against the veil. "Ponder that in the next world."

He stopped. He turned.

Tsukune stood, ignoring her wounds, readying Ofushikai in her practiced stance.

"One more," she said.

His confident expression faded. His eyes widened. He held up his blade and called out to the Hyōketsu. Again and again. Nothing. For the first time, his coal-fire eyes deadened with dawning realization.

"They won't hear you from Yomi," Tsukune said. "They are Phoenix now."

He spun to the tapestry. The dagger shook impotently. Nothing.

"No one is coming," she said. "You are by yourself, Ateru. Whereas I…"

Looking up at the rafters where a gossamer woman pointed at the fraying rope.

Noticing the tree in the garden, where an armored man crossed his arms.

A spectral hand on her shoulder when she almost touched the bone-hilted dagger.

A wise sensei urging her to cross the forbidden screen.

Shiba Ujimitsu's smiling face.

A dozen spectral forms unfurled around her. Their armored plates glowed with ethereal blue light, their shining blades reflecting on their serene faces. They each held a specter of Ofushikai. Like Phoenix Clan Champions.

She smiled. "…I am never alone."

His face twisted, his jaw distending with an animal roar. He lunged.

Her first strike knocked him aside. Her second shattered his dagger.

Her third cut him in two.

He screamed. Spectral blood, a splash of pearl against the ink, poured from his tear. As Tsukune followed through, a single droplet of his incandescent blood splashed into her right eye.

It was a white-hot shard, a spike driven into her socket. She gritted her teeth and blinked the lid, a trail of smoke snaking from beneath as she held her eye shut.

The battlefield rippled. Ateru jerked back, as if pulled in a riptide. His screams rattled Tsukune's teeth. With her good eye, she saw him pulled into that nightmarish tapestry beyond. Tōshigoku was finally claiming its own.

Then, he jerked forward and grabbed her kimono collar.

The current took her. She was being pulled in with him. She

fought, leaning back, straining, clenching. She smelled fire and heard the crash of battle. Where Ateru's skeletal fingers gripped, the fabric curled and burned.

"I won't go alone!" he shouted, his voice filling her head. There was no hatred or desire for vengeance. Just fear, raw and cold. "I'll drag you there too! I'll lash your soul to this realm! Unless you pull me back, unless—"

She leaned in. The current took them both.

He screamed. "You're insane! You'd willingly dive into that place?"

"If it will protect them from you, then absolutely." She looked into his confused eyes, her face serene and without regret. "My life, my soul, for the Phoenix."

As he screamed one final time, she closed her good eye, at peace with the world.

I cannot let you.

She opened her eye again. There was no current. She floated on the other side of the invisible veil. She was safe. But why?

And then she saw him. The glowing armor, the blue light, the serene face. Ujimitsu had tackled Ateru, throwing them both into the yawning void. Tōshigoku was hungry. It knew no difference between spectral dead.

His voice filled her mind one last time. *Thank you, Tsukune. Now my passing has purpose. Live on, and remind them what it means to be—*

The darkness swallowed them both. In her trembling hand, Ofushikai felt imperceptibly lighter.

As she floated numbly before the distant ethereal battleground, something stirred. She could not see it fully, for it was as if the planes were a painted lantern and the candle were slowly dimming. But she saw its silhouette, a massive suit of ebony armor, moving empty on its own. Two eyes, like lantern orbs, shone in the helm where its face should be, judging her. The hair on her forearms pricked up, and her heart waited to beat again. Guilt blanketed her soul.

Then its eyes softened. *No*, they seemed to say. *Not yet.*

Its gauntleted hand moved as if closing a shōji door. It, and the infinite battlefield, faded away.

One by one, the glowing champions collapsed into floating orbs. Like fireflies, they danced around the blade, casting their light against Tsukune's face. She watched them enter Ofushikai, melding with it like collecting mercury.

Ateru is gone, a voice said.

Another: *Tōshigoku is patient. It waited all this time.*

A third, more serene. *The Kaito's duty is complete now. The shrine is safe again.*

Tsukune let an air bubble give her a voice. "What of Ujimistu?"

There was a long silence.

Lost to us, a voice finally replied.

Despair pulled her eyes to the floor.

For now.

The last orb reabsorbed into the blade. As emptiness swelled in her chest again, Tsukune felt herself rising, limply, toward the surface of the well.

Tsukune pulled herself from the water with aching arms. Her tattered kimono clung wetly as she flopped to the shrine floor. Her hair formed a curtain around her face. The morning sun touched her skin, but she didn't feel it. She exhaled a stream and sat in a cold puddle, unmoving.

Six men formed a ring around her. They wore hooded cloaks emblazoned with a crest depicting an open eye. They held their naginata inches from her face, but made no motion to attack. They just watched.

Asako Maezawa stepped into the ring. "It's alright," he told them. "Stand down." He knelt beside her. "Tsukune-sama. What happened?"

She lifted her head. The curtain of hair parted from her face. They gasped. Tsukune's colorless right eye, flickering and translucent like a glowing orb, cast her face in a sickly light. Then, like a dying ember, the light faded.

"He's gone," she whispered limply. Her eyes swelled. "He's gone. He's gone."

Maezawa shook his head. "You poor child. What did they do to you?"

Realization broke her from her reverie. Beyond the ring, two others tended to Isawa Tadaka. He would not look at her. "Kosori!" he shouted. "He killed her. He—"

"Relax," Maezawa said reassuringly. "She lives."

Above her, the sky brightened.

He nodded. "It was close. Her spirit clung by only a thread. But I was able to save her."

She read his eyes. "You're not telling me everything."

His smile dampened. "The ghost. It…it touched her here, yes?" He gestured to his throat.

Tsukune's brow furrowed. "Why? What…what does that mean?"

Maezawa looked away.

Although it was morning, no matter how she strained, Tsukune could not hear the waking songs of the mountain birds.

Chapter Twelve

Tsukune spent three weeks in a bed facing away from the unlucky directions. Servants came every day, washing her wounds, applying healing herbs, and rebandaging. They gave her a straw-colored tea that tasted of barley. When the pain of her broken ribs stole her sleep, the servants drew her curtains and gave her *chandu* to smoke. It didn't make the pain didn't go away, but it made her stop caring and filled her with an energetic rush. At night they burned tea leaves and fennel in a burlap sack above her bed, until eventually, tired of the thick and smoke-filled air, she opened her window to let it out. When they discovered this, they said it was a good sign.

Most of all, they did not stare at her right eye, where her glossy iris had become a sickly purple. Each day her new reflection startled her less and less. She decided to wear her hair in a veil over the right side of her face. This seemed to make others more comfortable with it.

She tried walking again in the third week. Her joints were like planks, but soon she was performing her daily exercises, until finally the warden, distressed over the state of the floor mats, requested she try these outside.

By the shrine's precipice, construction of the new stone bridge was progressing swiftly. The scrapes and hammering of masons' tools resounded over the valley. It was a more expensive endeavor than the swinging bridge, but that was alright. Tsukune would ensure it didn't cost the Kaito anything.

There, she found Kosori. The girl was practicing her archery when Tsukune approached, a breeze seeming to lift the arrow to the target, dead center. Kosori whispered her thanks before realizing Tsukune was there. Her wide smile touched her shining eyes.

"Congratulations, Tsukune-san. You lived."

A shudder snaked down Tsukune's back. Pain rippled across Kosori's features when she spoke, her voice full of gravel and broken glass. It was barely more than a raspy whisper.

Pressure built in Tsukune's chest. Tears, bitter and hot, glossed her vision. Kosori's expression warmed, melting, and she shook her head urgently. She didn't want Tsukune to be upset.

But after this, how could Tsukune ever show her face to Kosori again? Kosori had loved to sing. It was her gift from the Fortunes. Hadn't Tsukune only been a curse to Kosori, when all Kosori had shown her was trust and kindness?

She looked away. "I'm sorry, Kosori. I…I ruined your life. I…"

Gentle hands on her shoulders. Kosori's eyes winced for a moment, no voice coming. But she mouthed the words, and Tsukune could hear them as clearly as if Kosori could speak.

"The art of archery is the art of letting go."

Shaking, Tsukune nodded. If Kosori did not hate her for this, then she supposed she shouldn't hate herself either. She stepped back, rubbed her face, and recomposed herself. "You're going to be a great daimyō, Lady Kosori." She paused. "Which is fortunate, because the Kaito family is receiving a new duty."

Kosori's brow furrowed. When Tsukune told her, she beamed and bowed low.

Asako Maezawa bowed as Tsukune left Kosori to resume her practice. "It is good to see you up and about, Tsukune-sama. I'm glad you did not make a liar of me."

"You do that well enough yourself," she replied.

He laughed. "Well, I've had a long time to practice."

She showed no amusement.

"You'll be well enough to ride a horse in another week or so," he remarked. "Your recovery was very fast. How is your arm?" He looked to her shoulder. "I am still amazed you didn't realize your collarbone was broken."

She extended her arm and made a fist. "It feels too slow. Stiff. I can't pull it back all the way."

"You should recover most of the motion. I'm afraid it may never be *quite* the same. But you'll always know when it's about to rain!" His smile never dropped. "All things considered, you are quite lucky. It could have been worse."

"Like Kosori, you mean."

He nodded. "The ki of the meridian was disrupted beyond my ability to restore. I did what I could."

"What of Tadaka?" Her voice cracked at his name. "He recovered?"

"Completely." Maezawa scratched his ear. "He left a few weeks ago to deliver his report to the council. He expressed regret that he had to leave so suddenly. He…he did ask me to watch over you. He wanted to say goodbye in person but…well."

"He could not show his face."

Maezawa looked away. "As you say, Tsukune-sama."

Two dragonflies danced along the cliffside fringe. She sighed at the pinprick in her heart. "He wanted so badly to prove the council wrong. I tried to help, but he just pushed me away."

"To be completely fair to him, I would not be here if we had not suspected Jigoku's forces were at work. Thankfully we were mistaken."

She regarded him sideways. "Who are 'we'? Some secret society within the Phoenix?"

"You could say that." His smile twitched. "Forgive my amusement that the council has not yet mentioned the Inquisitors in your presence. We watch for signs of corruption and act accordingly. Which naturally requires a certain degree of…discretion."

"How long have you been investigating Tadaka?" she asked.

The old man blinked. "Tadaka is not under investigation." He paused. "Should he be?"

She frowned. "You said there was a darkness within him."

"There is. Emotionally, he is quite burdened. It is obvious he cares a great deal about you, but now that things have changed for you both, he feels he must push you away. It is not healthy for him to be so dishonest about his feelings." He tilted his head. "What did you think I meant?"

"Never mind," she replied, cheeks reddening. Why didn't anyone ever speak plainly?

He shrugged. "In any case, we are grateful for your discovery. The histories of the Kaito will be quite useful to us. It is generous of Kosori to share them."

"I suspect the Kaito are done denying their past. A new wing will be erected in Cliffside Shrine for the worship of their oldest ancestors."

"There might be something in those documents for the council as well," he added. "It notes the exact date when the well began to thaw. It corresponds with when their waterfalls unfroze and the mountain climate became more hospitable to certain insect wildlife."

"The elemental imbalance," Tsukune concluded. "It's been happening for longer than we thought. The overactive fire kami is what melted the well and freed Ateru." She thought for a moment. "If the Kaito histories recorded this temperature change, why didn't they do anything?"

"They thought it was normal," Maezawa replied.

"Normal?"

Maezawa's splotchy eyes tilted to the cerulean sky. "Why wouldn't they? Anyone who remembers the well when it was frozen has long since retired. They are in monasteries or urns. Or else they're too stubborn for either." He chuckled. "In light of this, it makes sense that they would not recognize the warnings. It is the nature of man to proceed as if his actions have no consequences.

"That's the joke fate plays on mortals," he continued, meeting her gaze. "Even when old and withered, we are but children when fate takes us. Ten years to grow a tree, a hundred to produce a grove, and one thousand to educate a person. Only our experiences we treat as real. Anything else, we disregard." He looked back to the Heavens. "This world is merely the manifestation of the collective karma of all living beings, and karma is nothing more than consequences of thoughts and actions."

"Then you believe human beings are responsible for the elemental imbalance?" Tsukune asked. "That it is not a part of a natural cycle?"

"There is a natural cycle to the elements' rise and fall. But to say that our actions cannot impact the world is perhaps the haughtiest and most prideful thing I can think of." He sighed. "At least it worked out this time. Imagine if you were not here, Tsukune-sama. I dare not contemplate."

She stared at him for a long time.

"I should take your head," she whispered.

"You'd be justified," he agreed.

Her hand rested on her sword hilt. "You tried to kill us."

"You are within your rights. Go ahead."

He seemed frail. He was a candlewick that had burned too long.

"But know that I would do it again," he said. "I couldn't let him escape. If he did, he could have destroyed the Kaito. Would that satisfy his hatred? No. He would attack the villages. Would that sate him? No. He would attack the surrounding provinces. Then the Phoenix directly. Then the neighboring clans. And so on. People would die without knowing why, clutching to their confusion and hatred. How many more onryō would that create? How vast would Tōshigoku's numbers swell?" He shrugged. "Then again, perhaps not. Surely he would be defeated eventually. But I could not take that chance." He opened his palm and stared at the tattoo there, a wide-open eye. "The Asako's purpose is to heal. But sometimes, to save the body, one must cut off the arm. Thankfully, a severed arm can still grasp its sword.

"Anyway." Without looking at her, he pulled his collar, exposing his neck. "Do what your honor demands. I commit myself to the next life."

Tsukune's grip tightened. She was justified, wasn't she? The Kaito would have defeated Ateru. The old man didn't have to cut the bridge and trap them inside. In fact, he was ultimately why Kosori lost her voice. It was treason, plain and simple. Attempting to cause the death of a clan champion was unforgivable. She had every right to take his life. What was a samurai if not an instrument of karma? To kill him here would be justice. Fair and—

From whence come these thoughts?

She stopped. The knuckles of her sword hand were white.

Somewhere a bush warbler called and another answered. Her right eye was tearing up. She touched the wetness. At her fingertips rested droplets of glowing moonlight.

She uncurled her fingers from Ofushikai. "It would be a waste," she said. Maezawa drew out his pipe. They both watched the northern mountains rake the passing clouds.

"I'm making you my personal advisor," Tsukune decided.

Surprised, he bowed. "I am humbled, my lady. I'll serve you as best I can."

"You haven't gotten off easy." She plucked the pipe from his hands and leaned in closely. Showed him her sickly purple eye. "Your life is mine now, such as it is. You'd best stick around for a little while longer."

Tsukune left, taking the pipe with her.

Maezawa blinked in her wake. In the distance, Kosori's arrow struck the bell of Cliffside Shrine. The chime resounded throughout the valley.

He smiled. "At last, the Phoenix Clan Champion. I wondered if she was going to show up."

Epilogue

"They are ready."

Tsukune turned. Her brocaded silks and pale hakama invoked a flame dancing above a blessed candle, her kataginu proudly displaying the crest of the Phoenix Champion. "Lead on," she said. Tetsu nodded.

Soon they stood beneath a pagoda roof in the Garden of No Mind. The dancing grasses had become golden tipped as autumn painted the lands in new colors. They climbed the steps to the stone teahouse. Rain was falling in spite of the sun.

"Hm," Tetsu remarked. "A fox's wedding."

She glanced at him with a smirk. "That's right. A fox's wedding."

When they reached the top, Tetsu reached into his satchel and withdrew a thin bound stack of pages. Tsukune brightened when she saw it. "That's all of them?"

"All but a collection of letters, which I am still assembling." Tetsu offered her the stack. "Ujimitsu-sama wrote in this journal every day since he drew Ofushikai. It contains many of his deepest insights."

She accepted it with grateful hands. "Thank you." She ran her fingers across the weathered pages. "I want to learn everything I can about him. I will return it soon."

Tetsu flashed a smile. "Keep it. It is yours. Sensei would have wanted that."

Their gazes lingered together. Leaves fell from the ancient oak at the center of the Grove of the Five Masters.

"I'm sorry, Tetsu-san." Tsukune kept her eye on the pond. "I know I can never replace him."

He would not look at her.

"And I know you would rather it were you that was chosen. You are the better fighter, Tetsu. I need to work hard before I'll ever be at your level. I'm still not sure why the sword chose me." She looked to the sky. "But whatever the reason, I won't find it by hiding from my feelings, or trying to replace the others. I'm going to do things differently. I'm going to do my best." She smiled at him, the sunlight caught in her spectral eye. "How about you?"

Tetsu watched her enter the chamber of the Masters. "Me too," he whispered. "Me too."

The Masters took their seats as Tsukune entered. She approached confidently, stopping just beyond the lip of the table. Five Masters were here, Tsuke, Azunami, Eju…

No Rujo. The Earth Master was gone.

Seated in his place was Isawa Tadaka. His hands, fingers laced, rested on the stone table, his wide-brimmed conical hat nearly concealing his eyes. And there was something new: a crimson cloth wrapped around his face. On his chest was the jade-tinted crest of the Master of Earth.

Tsukune sighed. *I see.*

"Ah, Tadaka-san!" said Isawa Ujina as he sat beside his son. "I'm glad you could make it. I heard your caravan in Crab lands was delayed."

Tadaka's voice was only slightly muffled by the mask. "Temporary setbacks. I am used to them." He regarded her openly. "Hello, Tsukune. It has been some time."

"Congratulations on your recent appointment," she replied.

His eyes smiled.

"Now then," Ujina said, rapping the table with his cane. The Masters quieted. "You are the one who called this meeting, Champion.

What is this all about?"

As one, the Masters turned to her. Tadaka set his cheek on his hand, the amusement never leaving his eyes.

Taking a deep breath, she spoke.

"Honored Masters, recently unfolding events in Garanto Province have made clear the extent of the threat caused by the elemental imbalance. Our Empire is a garden where gods once walked, and as such, sacred places are without number. In light of what the fire imbalance unleashed in Cliffside Shrine, and knowing that many other shrines serve similar functions, I cannot imagine what else has been released."

"These are matters that the council has already considered," Tsuke replied.

Tsukune nodded. "I understand. I called this gathering to make clear my intentions." She met Tadaka's unflinching eyes. "I am launching my own investigation into the matter of the elemental imbalance. I have recruited the Kaito family for this purpose, as they have proven themselves in my eyes and won my confidence in this matter. Their orders are to investigate shrines, maintain the elemental order, and await the arrival of an Isawa shugenja to report their findings and set right whatever has been imbalanced. The Shiba family shall incur any unforeseen costs of this investigation, and it is my hope that by shouldering this duty, it will provide useful information for this council while freeing the Isawa from burdening distractions."

The Master of Water spoke. "This is not necessary, Tsukune-sama. This council and the Isawa have this matter well in hand. You needn't burden yourself."

"I am not asking permission. The Kaito have already begun."

Stunned silence prevailed for several moments.

"Outrageous!" Isawa Tsuke stood. "You have no such authority! The Kaito are an Isawa vassal."

"It does seem a little hasty," the Water Master agreed. "On what grounds did you believe you could do this?"

Tadaka watched her silently from the other side of the table. His eyes never left hers.

"My duty is to protect the Phoenix from all threats. The Phoenix's duty is to protect the Empire's spirit. A gardener who ignores their weeds dooms the garden. And so I have acted, and it is within my purview to do so." She lowered her head. "Even so, the Shiba bow to the Isawa, as always. I will stop if you so order." She let the light touch her spectral eye. "But only if."

Again, the chamber fell silent.

"Give her a chance," said Tadaka.

They all regarded him. His cheek still planted in his fist, he shrugged. "I see no reason to disallow a concurrent investigation. The Kaito are quite capable."

"It *could* provide useful information," Tsuke admitted.

The Water Master drummed her fingers. "Assuming knowledge of the existence of the elemental imbalance remains within the Phoenix until this council's approval to reveal it…" She leaned back. "Then I have no objections."

Tsuke crossed his arms. Then, after some time, he nodded.

"Then it is permitted," said Ujina. "The council wishes the Kaito great success in their new duty."

Tsukune bowed.

She saw him again that evening. She was sitting by the butterburs, composing a letter to the Crane Clan Champion, when his tall shadow raked the pink moss and fluttering grasses, cicadas keening in his wake. She wasn't certain if he'd seen her or not. Even though he was silhouetted, the crest of the Earth Master glowed on his back beneath the golden cracks of dusk's breaking.

And for a brief moment, she saw herself beside him. They were laughing. Younger.

That is not your path anymore.

She closed her eyes. *I know.* When she opened them, he was gone.

There is a piece of Tōshigoku with you now. It will serve you or become your master. Your trials have only started. And one day, your soul will join us. You will be a guide for whoever is next.

The sun torched the horizon. Where its shadows touched, Tsukune saw firelights blinking into being, like a thousand tiny lanterns. Separate, they were frail. Together, they lit the gardens in defiance of the night.

So be it, she thought. Her fingers curled around Ofushikai. *I am not afraid anymore.*

My life, my soul, for the Phoenix.

The Sword and the Spirits

About the Author

Robert Denton III lives in the New River Valley of Virginia with his wife and three cats. He is the author of over sixty short fictions for the *Legend of the Five Rings* universe and has contributed to several roleplaying books for the fourth edition of the *Legend of the Five Rings Roleplaying Game*, including *Secrets of the Empire* and *Imperial Histories 2*. Robert has also written for other roleplaying games such as *Tiny Frontiers* and its expansion *Mecha and Monsters*, and he is currently the Creative Lead for *Radiant: Offline Battle Arena*. *The Sword and the Spirits* is his first novella. You can visit him on Twitter: @ohnospooky

Legend of the Five Rings

THE CARD GAME

Enter the Emerald Empire

Rokugan

五輪伝

An Empire in Turmoil

A land where honor is stronger than steel. Here, the samurai of the seven Great Clans serve the Emperor as warriors, courtiers, priests, and monks. They live—and die—by the tenets of Bushidō.

The Elemental Council and untested champion of the Phoenix Clan struggle to discover the source of a great elemental disturbance. Perhaps the traditions of a small vassal family in the northern mountains may hold some clues...

THE LEGEND OF THE KAITO FAMILY

Near the dawn of the fifth century, a time of great strife for the Empire, a demon appeared in the lands of the Phoenix Clan. This demon terrorized the northern mountain range bordering Rokugan, desecrating shrines and destroying villages, and threw the entire Garanto Province into disarray. With the Pheonix's Clan Champion's attentions fixated on greater events in the Empire, it seemed that nothing could stop the demon. But then, a lone woman, with only her bow and the aid of the kami, confronted the demon on a tall mountaintop. Unflinching beneath the great beast's shadow, she slew the demon with her arrow, and then gave her life to trap its spirit, freezing it deep in the bottom of a well.

That woman was Isawa Kaito. She was an accomplished archer and priestess, and her teachings have informed many of the shrine-keeper traditions observed to this day. Her legendary battle with the demon saved the Garanto Province—and perhaps all of the Phoenix lands—from a terrible enemy. In honor of her sacrifice, her family was raised in status, becoming a vassal family of the Isawa. A shrine was erected at the battle site with the well at its center so that Kaito's descendants, continuing her unique traditions, could guard it and ensure that the demon would remain trapped. It is a duty the Kaito continue to observe today.

The Kaito are a tiny, rustic family of archer-mystics living in secluded mountain monastery among the Northern Wall Mountains in Garanto Province. Their holdings comprise their family estate, known as Sanpuku Seidō—Cliffside Shrine—and scattered villages within the surrounding valleys. Relatively isolated from the rest of the Phoenix and unknown to much of the Empire, the Kaito have developed their own unique practices in pursuit of their three duties to the clan. First, to train the clan's shrine keepers, second, to preserve their founder's techniques, and third, to protect their ancestral shrine from anything that might threaten it and release the evil trapped inside.

"I will launch my arrow
Over fog-lit peaks,
But ask my heart's true nature
And I freeze without reply."
– Garanto Province Song
attributed to Isawa Kaito

Sanpuku Seidō, Cliffside Shrine

Named for the sheer cliffs that precariously support its foundation, Cliffside Shrine is sacred and ancient, situated high above the Kaito Valley in Garanto Province, where winter rules for most of the year. It stands three days north of Kyūden Isawa, a dot of civilization on an unruly frontier. From its cliff, miles of Phoenix lands can be seen to the south, and to the north, distant signs of Yobanjin settlements are visible beyond the Imperial border. Sanpuku Seidō is the lone ancestral holding of the Kaito, enshrining not only their artifacts and histories, but also the ancient well in which Isawa Kaito trapped the demon known in the provincial dialect as an *ateru*. The origin of this well is unknown, but Isawa scholars postulate it is the last remaining artifact of a Tengu village that predated the Empire.

Nestled nearby is the Kaito estate, a monastery complex built on the side of a mountain. Little more than a cluster of towers clinging to a frosty cliff, this monastery houses most of the Kaito samurai. The complex boasts a number of humble living quarters, a small marketplace, a simple residence for the daimyō's family and guests, and a cave complex that wends its way deep into the mountains. The mountain is believed to be sacred, and all along the winding path up its slopes, one can find numerous smaller shrines and holy markers.

Here, the Kaito live simple, rustic lives. They are as self-sustaining as the frigid mountain will allow, growing a few hardy crops and foraging along the slopes. They take the rest of what they need from the scattered villages in the valleys beneath them. There, foresters, charcoal-burners, hunters, mushroom gatherers, and masons reside in *minka* farmhouses and thatched huts, all of which have steep-pitched roofs to protect against heavy snowfall. Even the peasants here are closely attuned to the spirits, recognizing the crucial give-and-take between the natural world and their own lives.

Far from towns and cities, the Kaito can perfect their archery and meditate on their founders' teachings. Few Kaito willingly stray from the place of their birth, although it is not unheard of for adherents of the shrine-keeper tradition to venture farther into the Empire for a time before returning, having learned new lessons. The isolation of the Kaito is explicitly encouraged by the daimyō of each generation. The distractions of the civilized world are seen as a detriment to each family member's inward pursuit: to become one with the kami through the practice of archery. The Kaito aspire to become "living shrines" in which the kami can freely dwell. In this way they hope to emulate their founder and enter into harmony with the true nature of the universe.

THE KAITO FAMILY MON

As the Kaito family is a vassal of the Isawa, its *mon* is derived from the Isawa crest. It depicts a five-pointed star, symbolizing the interconnections among the five elements and the cycles of change and transformation of earthly life. Within the center of this star is a circle, symbolizing the well in which Kaito trapped the demon, as well as the moon, for which the ancestral bow of the Kaito, Mikazuki, is named.

The Kaito Shrine-Keeper Tradition

Within the monastery complex is a humble, square-shaped dōjō enclosing a small shrine. This is the Dōjō of the Swaying Branch, the Kaito Shrine-Keeper School. It is in this place's quiet halls, cloistered garden, subterranean caverns, and mountainside archery range that students train in the ways of the shrine keeper and priest.

The shrine keeper serves an important role in the upkeep and protection of a shrine. They live in the shrine, tend to the needs of the spirits dwelling there, keep the shrine purified, and ensure its safety. They are also responsible for organizing the maintenance of shrine buildings, which entails the customary replacement of roofs and walls every generation as well as the proper disposal of the old materials and consecration of the new ones. When another priest or a *shugenja* attends a shrine, it is the responsibility of the shrine keeper to assist them in any rituals or ceremonies. In the absence of a priest, it is the shrine keeper's duty to undertake these ceremonies themself, as is common at many of Rokugan's more rural shrines.

This requires a set of specialized skills and training. A shrine keeper must be able to assist visitors without impeding their worship, commune with the shrine's spirits, and maintain the balance of the sacred place. An encyclopedic knowledge of the different types of spirits and the characteristics of the various Spirit Realms is essential, as is familiarity with divination, wards of protection and banishment, and ceremonial offerings and, on occasion, the exorcism of malicious spirits and even demons.

The Training of a Shrine Keeper

The Dōjō of the Swaying Branch accepts only a handful of applicants each year. Anyone of the samurai caste with an adequate recommendation may apply, but the school only accepts those who pass their initial inspection This is because the Kaito's teachings include far more powerful mysteries and techniques than those traditions practiced by peasant laity and shrine keepers.

Members of the Isawa family born without the shugenja gift are common applicants, as are Shiba and Asako whose families need fresh shrine keepers. Even students from other clans may be accepted if they go through the proper channels. Acceptance into the school is not limited to a single gender. Female graduates are called *miko*, and others are called *geki*, but their training and positions are identical. Those lucky enough to be chosen are sent to live at Cliffside Shrine in the frosty mountains, where they can awaken to the spirit world without the distractions of civilization. If they complete their six years of training, they become full-fledged shrine keepers, ready to serve and protect any of Rokugan's countless shrines.

The most successful shrine keepers possess a natural affinity with sacred places and a rapport with the kami. Although they lack the abilities of true shugenja, they can still sense the moods of the kami and enjoy benefits of their favor. These manifest in different ways, such as a natural affinity with animals, an inability to become lost or without direction, or a tendency to experience brief visions of events long past. The most devout shrine keepers may even serve as oracles or mediums for spirits. Although they are unable to communicate directly with the kami as the shugenja do, they can become living conduits for the kami's messages. What truly sets a shrine keeper apart is twofold and intertwined: their martial prowess with the bow, and their ability to become possessed by the kami, who lend their arrows supernatural attributes.

Beyond their spiritual studies, shrine keepers learn to defend their sacred spaces through the art of archery, *kyūjutsu*, as well as to use archery techniques to help them become empty vessels in which the kami can dwell. Even when they are beginners, their archery is unnervingly accurate, as though their hands are guided by invisible spirits. As they advance within their school, they learn the secrets of imbuing arrows with spiritual qualities and the blessings of particular kami. These enchantments allow them to defend their sacred places from malicious *yōkai* such as ghosts, demons, and even monsters.

SHRINE KEEPERS ACROSS ROKUGAN

The duty of the shrine keepers is to protect shrines, sacred places, and visiting pilgrims. Every well-maintained shrine in Phoenix lands can boast at least one Kaito-trained shrine keeper on the premises. However, due to the Kaito's small numbers, Kaito-trained shrine keepers are a rare sight beyond Phoenix borders, and only well-versed shugenja are likely to recognize them. Even so, shugenja and shrine keepers from other clans who encounter them quickly learn to respect their expertise.

While most miko and geki receive assignments directly from the Kaito daimyō (as requests for a knowledgeable shrine keeper are not uncommon), some observe a tradition that began with Isawa Kaito's youngest daughter, Kaito Maruko. After graduation, a keeper following this tradition climbs to the hazardous peak of Garanto Mountain, risking many dangers to reach the snow-swept summit. There, the keeper meditates for three days. Then, when their heart and mind are in accord, they fire a single arrow. It is said that the kami themselves carry the arrow to wherever that shrine keeper's destiny lies. The keeper seeks the arrow for weeks or even months until they find where it landed.

Often this journey takes them beyond the borders of Garanto Province. In one documented case, a shrine keeper's arrow stuck unnoticed into the palanquin of an Imperial princess visiting Phoenix lands. The miko, eventually tracking the arrow to the Imperial City itself, became the princess's personal spiritual guide and protector. This tradition has given rise to a superstition among Garanto peasants over the years: if a person ever finds an arrow sticking up from the ground, leave it be—to pluck it from the earth would be to invite a terrible calamity.

The Kami Arrow

The tribes who dwelled in Rokugan before the Fall of the Kami considered the bow to be a sacred weapon. It was said that a plucked bowstring could banish demons, and sacred arrows were used to invoke rain and divine the future. Arrow divination was practiced by many of the scattered tribes predating Rokugan, including the Tribe of Isawa. After the formation of the Phoenix Clan, many of those tribes retreated deeper into the northern mountains, and the Isawa Tribe's tradition of arrow divination were gradually replaced by other techniques. The Kaito still keep these traditions alive, however, venerating the bow and utilizing the art of archery as a means to become more suitable vessels for the spirits.

At first glance, the Kaito's embrace of a martial art is quite unusual, seeming to violate the pacifistic principles of a family so close to the kami. Indeed, most shugenja eschew such weapons, as there is little synergy between the arts of death-dealing and the path of the kami, the very embodiment of life. Every life taken by a shugenja weakens their connection to the kami, and so shugenja only resort to violence when there is no other option.

MIKAZUKI, THE CRESCENT MOON BOW

Enshrined within Sanpuku Seidō is the *yumi* once carried by Isawa Kaito herself: Mikazuki, the ancestral bow of the Kaito. Like most yumi, the bow is asymmetrical and taller than its wielders. It is made of laminated bamboo and catalpa wood, wrapped in rattan, and adorned with silk tassels and a silver bell. To the unknowing, it might appear to be purely ornamental, but even before it fell into the hands of the Phoenix, Mikazuki was an awakened object, or *nemuranai*, and a vessel for a kami. A single pluck of its bowstring can disrupt or pacify malicious spirits, and any arrow it launches is sacred, and therefore harmful to evil beings. Legends say the bow can also freeze water with an arrow, although the knowledge of how to do this was lost with Isawa Kaito.

Only the rightful Kaito daimyō can string Mikazuki. For all others, the string will snap or the bow will refuse to bend. The Kaito use this both to establish the succession line of their daimyō and to let the daimyō prove their own worthiness. Only once in its history has the bowstring snapped in the hands of the Kaito daimyō, resulting in that daimyō's voluntary retirement to some distant monastery.

HEARTS OF ICE

While many of Rokugan's archery traditions associate the bow with the Air or Void Element, to the Kaito, the bow is aligned with Water. It is a flexible weapon—the bowstring is as a calm pool until an arrow is loosed with the ferocity of a waterfall. The the gentleness with which the wielder must treat the weapon is attributed to the nature of Water, and so the Kaito seek to become as Water. When mixed with Air, the family's secondary element, water freezes. As ice, the Kaito are sharp, unyielding, and crystal clear in their intentions.

Both elements are central to the Kaito's philosophy and outlook on life. Their doctrine and training centers on when it is appropriate to be receptive to the kami, as water, and when they must steel their heart against the predations of yōkai, as ice. Outsiders will sometimes wonder at the manner of the Kaito, warm and friendly in one instant, then icy cold and emotionless in the next. Yet this is simply their way.

A careful balance of the extremes is required, but the Kaito must not dwell too long in between. Ice is inflexible, while water can be formless.

However, to the Kaito, archery is not a violent art, and the bow is not a tool exclusively used for fighting. Unlike other weapons, for which agility, haste, and strength are principal virtues, the bow teaches softness and patience. The yumi is inherently fragile; it is ruined if mistreated and breaks if drawn incorrectly. Impatient warriors will snap bowstrings or crack the laminated bamboo of the bow, while overzealous archers will run out of stamina before the bow is fully drawn. To fire an arrow successfully, one must adopt a different mind-set, one that the Kaito recognize as properly conditioning oneself for unity with the kami. To the Kaito, kyūjutsu is more than just the art of firing an arrow: it is the primary means by which they become living vessels in which the kami may dwell. In other words, when Kaito shrine keepers draw their bow, they become possessed by the kami, and when they release the arrow, it is the kami who guide it.

This accounts for the Kaito school's emphasis on technique and ritual. In order to become a kami vessel, one must become aligned with nature, and the mind must empty. There are many ways for miko and geki to achieve this, but due to their traditions and duty to the clan, the Kaito have chosen archery. To assist them in this goal, their kyūjutsu school teaches them additional techniques, such as mindful breathing, correct posture, meditative mantras, and the affixing of charms and prayers to arrows.

This can make a Kaito archer seem mystical compared to archers from other schools. Ultimately, however, kyūjutsu is the art of shooting targets, and the Kaito school is no different. Its students' means of drawing and firing are the same as at any other archery school in Rokugan; any differences in archery are purely philosophical and stylistic. In the end, Kaito kyūjutsu is still kyūjutsu,

albeit a martial tradition where the archery is assisted by the kami.

While possessed, Kaito archers can imbue their arrows with special properties. A mundane arrow might take on the sacred properties of jade, or change direction unexpectedly, or make a whistling sound without having a humming-bulb tip. Legends speak of greater feats, such as creating arrows that strike like thunderbolts, melt armor, or pass through flesh but snag the soul, tearing the spirit away from the body and pinning it to the ground. Kaito archery masters have not publicly claimed these otherworldly abilities in recent memory, but the testimonies of their venerated ancestors are not untrue. All Kaito ultimately aspire to be capable of such works, rising above the material world and becoming one with the kami through their art.

Kaito archery is not meant for mortal targets. Instead, the Kaito deploy their skills against invading spirits and sources of spiritual impurity. To keep their art pure, shrine keepers vow never to use their archery against human targets, some going so far as to swear off shooting at anything considered living. The act of killing is inherently distressing, enough to bring an archer out of the serene mind-set necessary for the kami to dwell within.

Even so, history recalls some Kaito who were so at peace with the natural world that such trivialities were no obstacle to them when it came to the defense of the Phoenix. As these Kaito used their art purely in defense of threatened shrines, Asako histories absolve them, referring to them as the "Icy Hearts of the Kaito." And of course there is the matter of Isawa Kaito herself, who was not above using her bow to do what was necessary…

Customs of the Kaito Family

The Kaito family's customs are distinct from those of the rest of the Phoenix Clan, which is partly due to their isolation in the northern mountains.

THE KAITO AND THE KAMI

The Kaito are not a true shugenja family. While a few each generation are born with the kami's gift (and are subsequently taken under the Isawa's wing), most have no innate ability to speak with the kami and cause them to manifest. Instead, the Kaito enjoy a different relationship with the kami, one that is less potent and less directly powerful, but still very real.

Isawa Kaito was close to the world of spirits. At certain hours, she could even see them, or so Phoenix histories attest. The kami were naturally drawn to her, amused and enthralled by her mere presence, and they were eager to bestow upon her their blessings. Kaito encouraged this relationship with offerings and whatever demonstrations seemed to please them. While she could not invoke the kami or cause them to manifest in the same way that shugenja can, her closeness to the spirit world made her a vessel in which the kami could dwell. By emptying herself and becoming one with nature, she could become temporarily possessed by the kami, allowing her to perform seemingly impossible feats.

When she finally passed from the world, the kami she befriended remained with her bloodline. They see no difference between Kaito and her children. They still follow them as they followed her, still amused, eager to bestow their blessings.

This is how the priesthood of the Kaito family differs from that of true shugenja. While shugenja deliberately invoke the kami and beseech them to manifest, the Kaito make themselves vessels for the kami. While this is not as visually impressive or distinctive as a shugenja's invocations, kami possession does allow the Kaito to excel in physical tasks, becoming keenly perceptive, unnervingly calm, supernaturally active, or able to endure harsh conditions. Most importantly, kami possession aligns one's *ki* with that of the Spirit Realms, allowing one to interact with even ethereal denizens of those realms. In essence, the end goal of a member of the Kaito school is to become a living shrine in which the kami can freely dwell. Such masters of Isawa Kaito's technique are cold, graceful, and serene, perfectly aligned with the natural world.

Unlike the "magic" of shugenja, which requires an innate and rare gift, the Kaito's techniques theoretically can be taught to anyone, although they come easier to those sharing a natural connection to the kami. Elsewhere in Rokugan, other samurai priests have developed their own techniques for treating with their local kami and maintaining their shrines and sacred places. Yet, just as Isawa samurai are the archetypal shugenja, the Kaito are the archetypal shrine keepers.

Concerning childbirth, Kaito temper their joy over new life with hard-learned caution. The Kaito have many birthing superstitions, as both the parent giving birth and child are very close to death when the new life comes into the world. Whenever possible, a shugenja is in attendance, divining for the child's kami affinity mere hours after birth. A newborn who shows signs of great elemental aptitude is surrendered to the Isawa family without incident, owing to an ancient agreement between Isawa Kaito and the Elemental Masters. All others are simply blessed in accordance with Isawa traditions.

It is not uncommon among the Kaito for a newborn's grandparents to divine the child's path in life. To do this, the child is made to grasp an arrow, which their grand-

THE VILLAGE PARABLE

Imagine a village. In this village lives a dog. The dog has no master, yet its presence benefits the village in many ways, keeping away harmful predators and alerting townsfolk when something is wrong. While none would mistake the dog for human, it is as much a part of the village as any other villager. For its part, the dog does not understand the behavior of the villagers and does not even think in such terms. It merely acts as a dog acts.

There is a man living in this village. He is prestigious and important, and wields much influence. Sometimes he will go to the field and call for the dog. When he does, the dog will come. The man offers the dog treats, and in exchange, the dog performs whatever tricks and tasks the man requests. Sometimes the man has the dog fetch him something, or he asks the dog to follow him for a while.

The dog does not know why the man desires him to do these things, but that doesn't matter so long as the man continues to reward him.

Also in this village is a woman. She is not as influential as the man, nor as prestigious, but she has a beautiful and true heart. Whenever the dog sees her, it runs eagerly to her side. It bounces around her, following her everywhere, performing tricks, hoping to please her. It does not expect any treats or rewards for these tricks. It just likes her. It wants to be near her, to make her smile, to aid and protect her. And although she cannot command the dog and has no control over it, she trusts that the dog will never harm her. That is the nature of their relationship.

The village is the natural world. The dog is the kami. The man is the Isawa shugenja. And the woman is the Kaito shrine keeper.

parent later releases at a target to the southwest. A number of things can be divined based on how the arrow lands, such as the child's future prospects, their health, and what challenges they may face in life. The arrow, referred to as a *jinsei-no-ya*, or life arrow, is given to the parents to commemorate their child's entry into life. It is kept at the family shrine until that child's *gempuku*, or coming-of-age ceremony.

GEMPUKU

Kaito gempuku traditions vary greatly from those of the Isawa due to their lack of true shugenja. Before gempuku, Kaito children are considered genderless and "children of the kami." Therefore, the intended goal of a Kaito's coming-of-age ceremony is not only to prove that they are worthy of a place within the family, but also to help them retain some connection to the spirit world that might otherwise be lost upon entering the gendered world of adults.

The Kaito refer to the coming-of-age ceremony as *shufuku*, meaning "the first service." A Kaito undergoing this ritual is tested on archery, spirit identification, ward creation, and general knowledge of shrines and ceremonies, all under the supervision of sensei and the family daimyō. The final event is a pledge of loyalty and duty, followed by a plunge into icy water. After emerging, the student is presented with their adult clothing and a brush, with which they write their newly chosen adult name into the family genealogy. It is believed this plunge will permanently attract one of the many local water kami, who will follow the student for the duration of their life.

The new Kaito also receives a bow, often handed down from a grandparent, along with the life arrow created at their birth. The passing of this arrow symbolizes that the responsibility for that Kaito's welfare, and the perpetuation of Kaito traditions among their descendants, is now theirs.

COURTSHIP AND MARRIAGE

The Kaito are a rustic and simple folk, and their views on courtship are far more relaxed than the Isawa's, owing in part to the lowered emphasis on the hereditary gift of speaking to the kami. They have fewer courtship traditions than other families. Romantic love is considered a gift and an expression of the kami's joy. As long as it is not perceived as clouding one's judgment, there is no shameful connotation to loving openly. Subtle public displays of affection, while not exactly welcomed, are typically ignored unless truly disruptive. Whatever comes naturally is generally accepted to be harmonious.

Arranged marriages are still common, however. The Kaito prefer to match childhood friends based on compatibility and propitious star signs. Unlike many families in Rokugan, the Kaito do not consider it shameful to request a specific match, although if it is declined, that is expected to be the end of the matter.

As the Kaito are a lesser family of the Phoenix, other families rarely marry into it. The few exceptions to this rule are the spouses of the Kaito family daimyō, their children, and honored sensei. Otherwise, if a Kaito is not marrying another Kaito, Kaito samurai take the family name of the spouse they are marrying.

FUNERALS

The Kaito's closeness to the spirit world lends them a more accepting view of death. They know it to be a part of the natural cycle, merely a step toward the rebirth of the soul into a new form. Even so, the death of a Kaito is a somber occasion, filled with many quiet rites to ensure the peaceful transition of the departed. The elements of Kaito funerals follow typical Rokugani tradition, with a few notable exceptions. For one, the family of the recently deceased remains completely silent throughout the ceremony and after. They do not wear overcoats, instead enduring the cold of the mountain. Additionally, floating paper lanterns are set adrift over the mountains to guide the departed to the next world.

Marking the end of the Kaito funeral is the release of the departed's life arrow. A small sachet containing some of the ashes of the departed is affixed just behind the arrowhead, and then the arrow is released to wherever the kami take it. It is believed that the farther north one can shoot the arrow, the easier it will be for the departed spirit to leave this world behind. For this reason, the arrow's launch is entrusted to an accomplished family member or sensei. If something goes awry, such as the bowstring breaking, or if the shot is fouled, it is considered a dire omen, and the departed's entire family extends their silence for weeks in atonement for whatever unspoken shame caused the problem.

SUPERSTITIONS

The Phoenix hold more spiritual customs than any other clan, and the Kaito are no exception. Like most Phoenix, they consider supernatural signifiers to be irrefutable messages from the kami. Also like typical Phoenix, they tend to accept the superstitions of other families without question, taking them at face value and observing them reverently. This is due to the Kaito's incorporation of local folk beliefs into their curriculum and lore; even the strangest local superstition might one day be the key to a shrine's safety, and it would not do to offend unseen spirits.

Unsurprisingly, the Kaito hold a number of archery-related superstitions. For instance, a Kaito will never lean their bow against a living tree, as this is believed to sap the bow of its spirit. When a bowstring snaps in practice, this is believed to be good luck, and the archer should wait a day before restringing so that the bow can rest. Finally, when firing arrows, one should always drop the fourth one, continuing with the fifth. Indeed, the entire Kaito archery tradition could be considered superstitious, as the Kaito embrace a more spiritual practice of the art.

Frozen Memories:
The Secret Shame of the Kaito

The Kaito family founding is a lie, and Isawa Kaito was not at all what she seemed. The truth of the Kaito's founding is a deeply concealed secret, one that is not known by most members of the family. Only the Kaito daimyō and a few others, including the Council of Elemental Masters, know the truth about Isawa Kaito. The Phoenix keep this secret out of respect for what she gave the clan, and to save face for her descendants.

Isawa Kaito, born Kaito no Momotsukihime, was the high priestess and princess of a Yobanjin tribe known as the Hyōketsu. She was a medium and augurer with great reverence for the kami and a number of sacred gifts. Her people were among those who would not bow to Hantei at the dawn of the Empire, but their rivalry with the Isawa Tribe had begun long before that. They considered the Isawa to be their ancient enemies, owing to a slight that had divided them. When they retreated north, they took their traditions with them, including their archery divinations and rituals.

Although Kaito was respected among her people, she was but one of the Hyōketsu's three leaders. The first was her father, the chieftain, and the second was the foremost warrior of the tribe and her betrothed, an ambitious man known as Ateru. Kaito had no love for Ateru, seeing him as cruel and uncaring, but to follow tradition and keep the peace of the tribe, she rarely opposed him.

At the turn of the fifth century, her people fell on hard times. Drought and famine pushed them into desperate raids against the Empire to the south, raids that were fueled by their ancient rivalry with the Isawa. The Phoenix military forces being preoccupied with greater matters, the raids were successful, and Ateru was encouraged to stage increasingly ambitious attacks. Kaito reluctantly agreed to the raids because she believed they had no choice. However, as Ateru's raids grew into an extended campaign to steal the wealth of the Isawa and expand Hyōketsu territory, she started to regret her role in this decision.

As time passed and Ateru's military victories grew, Kaito began to despise the actions of her tribe. The sacred archery traditions, meant to honor the kami, were instead deployed against helpless Rokugani commoners. She watched her people pillage shrines, desecrate sacred ground, and burn fields of grain. The destruction of each shrine was an icy dagger in her heart, and she felt the anguish of the kami with each of Ateru's victories. Daily she prayed for guidance, wishing that she had never consented to the destruction. War had changed her people, and she hated what they had become.

When the Phoenix warriors finally confronted the Yobanjin harrying Isawa lands, trapping Ateru's forces at a mountain pass, Kaito knew it would be the end of the Hyōketsu, and that Ateru would not see reason or surrender. Perhaps the Rokugani would not even accept such a gesture. In that moment, as Ateru prepared to turn the tide and confront the Phoenix directly, Kaito realized she had a choice: allow her people to slowly die off to counterattacks and Ateru's ambition, or reach out to the very people they had been raiding and relinquish her culture in the process. To save the few who were loyal to her and end the suffering of the land, Kaito decided to betray the Hyōketsu, her family and her very people, to their enemies.

Under darkness, taking the handful she knew to be most loyal to her, she approached the Phoenix Clan in secret, asking to parlay with its leaders. She made them an offer: accept her and her followers' offer of fealty to the Phoenix, and she would deliver Ateru to them without resistance. The Elemental Masters saw the wisdom of the plan, which would minimize the bloodshed and risk for the Phoenix. They accepted the Yobanjin princess's plan. The dawn saw a massacre of the Hyōketsu at the hands of Shiba family warriors. Among the bodies, Ateru's was not found.

Nevertheless, Kaito was granted the Isawa name and given a small estate in the mountains of Garanto Province. As she possessed some affinity with the kami, it was rationalized that Kaito was surely a lost member of the Isawa. They gave her an Isawa husband and granted her the fiefdom of the surrounding lands, allowing her people to worship as she saw fit. It was not much, but she had managed to save a handful of loyal followers, and the traditions of her people would live on.

Kaito ruled there for many years. She had a number of children and taught them her techniques, which would become the foundation of the Kaito shrine-keeper traditions. For the sake of creating a future for her followers, Kaito asked them to live as the Rokugani did, which they reluctantly did. She sought to preserve what she could of the Hyōketsu ways by weaving them into Rokugani belief. Her true lineage was suppressed, her true origins forgotten. With time, few would remember that the Kaito were once Yobanjin. For a time, they knew peace.

However, as successful as she was, Kaito knew she would one day have to pay for her betrayal. One cannot take back a loosed arrow. She'd betrayed not only her family, but her entire people, perhaps most the very ones whom she had saved by forcing them to abandon their way of life. That day eventually came when, shortly after Kaito's eldest daughter's gempuku, Ateru returned. Wielding his signature bone dagger, Ateru incited an insurrection among those dissatisfied with life among the Rokugani. Soon the valley erupted into rebellion, with Ateru leading forces against those still loyal to Isawa Kaito.

Kaito knew this was her fate, and she'd prepared for this moment since she had first approached the Isawa. She sent her husband and children away and invited her enemies to strike her on sacred ground, choosing to make her stand by the sacred well where the water kami were strongest. Alone, using all her talents and martial skill and the will of the kami, she sacrificed herself to destroy Ateru and the renegades.

As Kaito lay dying, she realized that Ateru's dagger had become an artifact of Tōshigoku, the Realm of Slaughter. Ateru's spirit would not rest: it would try to destroy her family for the rest of time. And so, with her last breath, she prayed to the kami to seal his body in the well, freezing the water to imprison the hatred that had consumed his soul. None were present to know whether Kaito died with regrets about the arrow she had loosed those decades ago.

When word reached the Isawa, they were impressed. This was proof that the martial art Kaito had developed, one that mingled mortal and kami together, was effective in protecting their sacred lands. And so, the Isawa embraced her teachings and granted her family vassal status. Its members' sworn duty was to cultivate the arts of the shrine keeper and to protect the shrine at which she'd made her final stand. The Kaito's traditions were close to the original shamanism practiced by the Isawa Tribe, so the Isawa family had no objection to the preservation and teaching of Kaito traditions—especially as they benefited the Phoenix Clan.

To most of the Empire, and also to most of the Phoenix, only Kaito's last stand is well known. A famous travel diary by her daughter Tsuruko, written in the wake of her mother's death, states that Kaito was born a peasant of the Isawa and worked her way up to the position of priestess. In some ways, this account is correct, and few have the knowledge to object to it. The peasants of the Kaito still whisper of a barbarian princess who led them to this land, but the idle talk of peasants is hardly a matter any upstanding samurai would accept over official documents. The true lineage of Isawa Kaito was willfully forgotten.

Still, Shinsei once warned that three things are not long hidden: the sun, the moon, and the truth. One day, the frozen story will be thawed and a new arrow loosed. The Kaito will show their strength on that day, or be lost forever.